Dove Cottage

Dove Cottage

–

Jan Hilliard, *pseud. 3*
Hilda Kay Grant

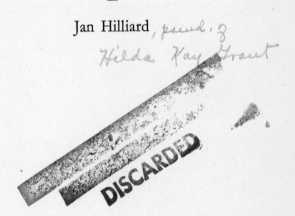

DISCARDED

Abelard-Schuman
London New York

Printed in Great Britain by
The Camelot Press Ltd, London and Southampton
for Abelard-Schuman Ltd, 38 Russell Square, London WC1
and 404 Fourth Avenue, New York 16

Chapter One

ONE day in February Homer Flynn received a letter from the legal firm of Ramsay, Claxton and Stone, requesting that he get in touch with them regarding the will of his late aunt, Harriet Jeffries.

He had been expecting such a letter for many weeks. His aunt Harriet had died months before, but because she had left no will the estate could not be settled until a search had been made for possible heirs. She had run a boarding house, and though Homer didn't suppose she had ever made more than enough money to supply her own needs, she had owned the house, a monstrous, extremely ugly and run-down mansion on a street that had been fashionable fifty years ago but now was lined with houses of ill repute. On spring evenings gaily painted ladies strolled up and down under the budding chestnuts and flowering magnolia trees.

Homer believed that, despite its location on Lavinia Street, his aunt Harriet's place was a perfectly respectable boarding house, the young ladies it sheltered—strangers to the city—being unaware of what was going on next door. Aunt Harriet herself went to church twice every Sunday, and her rather dingy reception hall, with its chandelier of clouded glass and its thready stair carpet, was hung with framed mottos such as "Love One

Another" and "Bless This House." But Homer was ashamed of her, just the same, and none of his friends knew he had an aunt living on Lavinia Street. He had never really liked her, though he did pity her. He felt that she must be very lonely in that dismal house, shut up in the two back rooms that she reserved for her own living quarters. Compassion, and the hope of falling heir to her insurance, had impelled him during the latter years of his aunt's life to visit her every third Sunday afternoon, taking along an inexpensive gift such as a half-pound box of chocolates. His wife had rarely accompanied him on these trips to Lavinia Street. His mother-in-law, being an inquisitive type, had once visited his aunt on a week-day afternoon, receiving such a cool reception that she had returned home in a huff, and for days afterwards made disparaging remarks about Homer's family tree.

Homer was, so far as he knew, his aunt Harriet's sole living relative. She had been widowed for years. Her only son, Claude, had run away from home when he was fifteen. A number of items belonging to his mother and her boarders had disappeared at the same time. These included a diamond ring valued at three hundred dollars, a cultured pearl necklace, a watch, a five dollar gold piece, a ruby pendant, two hundred dollars he had found in a cash box under his mother's bed, sums of money ranging from two to forty dollars from each of the boarders, and a suitcase. His mother had never heard from him again, but years later she had received through the mail an envelope containing a number of newspaper clippings which reported that he had drowned while attempting to go over Niagara Falls in a barrel. Claude had exhibited such black-sheep tendencies that both his mother and Homer accepted the news of his passing without question and without regret. Both had been trying for years to ignore his existence. After his death they pretended that he had never lived.

When his aunt finally died, Homer gave her a very decent funeral, using part of his own savings. He hoped to recoup this loss; in fact, he had high hopes of inheriting a few thousand dollars, perhaps even enough to buy a house in the country for his retirement. At the bank where he worked the retirement age was sixty-five. He had ten more years to go, but unless his aunt left him something, he didn't see how he was going to manage on the small pension he would receive.

Homer lived with his wife, Dolly, and his mother-in-law, Mrs. Vera Bigelow, in a three-room flat over a tobacco shop on Elm Street. The living room was furnished with a flowered blue Wilton carpet, three red over-stuffed chairs, an imitation fireplace, a bookcase filled with paperbacks, a small chest of drawers, a bed that pulled out of the wall, and a ten-inch television set on a corner table. When visitors came, Homer had to reach into the dining alcove and draw one of the hard oak chairs around for his own use. Every time the people in the flat upstairs pulled the toilet chain, conversation in the Flynn's living room was suspended for some minutes, until the gushing and gurgling in the water pipes subsided.

Dolly's younger sister Grace lived in the flat across the hall. Grace's husband, Raymond Collins, was a war hero on a pension. He had lost a foot during the war, and this disability, plus sundry ailments which doctors were unable to diagnose, made it difficult for him to keep a job. He had tried everything, from selling insurance to adding up figures in a brokerage house. Winters were hardest on him. Since November he had been too unwell to do anything but lie around the flat all day, waiting for Grace to come home from her job in an advertising agency so that he could tell her how much he had suffered during her absence.

The letter from Ramsay, Claxton and Stone arrived in the morning's mail, and lay unopened on the bookcase, along with the gas bill and two seed catalogs that Homer had ordered some weeks earlier, until he returned home at a quarter to six. Dolly was in the kitchen warming up last night's pot roast and baking a pie. She dropped everything when she heard his key in the lock. "There's a letter for you, Homer, on the bookcase." She stood looking over his shoulder while he slit the envelope and read the brief message.

"It's from those lawyers, about Aunt Harriet's estate. They must have got it settled at last."

"And about time, too."

"They want me to go to see them. As soon as possible, they say."

"Will you go tomorrow?"

"Tomorrow first thing."

"How much do *you* think she's left us, Homer?"

"Well, it all depends on whether they've found another heir, and I don't see how they could have. If Aunt Harriet had any other relatives—living ones, that is—I never heard of them."

"Would she have left as much as five thousand, do you think?" This was the figure Dolly had arrived at in her own mind, during endless daydreams. She had already decided that one of their first purchases would be a new television set. The old one was so small the entertainers looked like midgets.

"More than that. Remember she owned the house.

Mortgaged, probably, but even so. . . . Ten thousand," Homer said recklessly.

"I'll say five, then I won't be disappointed."

"We'll go on a binge, a real tooter. I'll get tickets for a play, and afterwards we'll go to one of those night clubs."

"Mother, too?" Dolly asked.

"Your mother, too," Homer agreed. "And Grace and Raymond. It'll be a nice treat for them."

Mrs. Bigelow, who had been window-shopping down town, was soaking her feet in the bathroom. She sat on the rim of the tub with her skirts hiked up over her knees. Dolly's mother was seventy-two, but young for her years. She kept abreast of the times, got a new how-to-do-it book from the library every two weeks: *How to Make Money in Your Spare Time, How to Play the Mandolin, How to be a Social Success*. She had already mastered the mandolin—an old one she had picked up at a church bazaar—and could play six songs. What she really wanted was to take up landscape painting and be like Grandma Moses, but could not afford to buy the materials, for she hadn't a cent beside her old age pension. Being poor was hard on her, since she had once known better days.

"You want to use the bathroom, Homer?" She poked her head around the half-open door and shouted over the water gushing into the tub.

Homer didn't bother answering. He went into the bedroom to change into his at-home clothes: a white cotton jersey, gray flannel trousers with the knees coming through, and brown sneakers.

Mrs. Bigelow pulled the plug in the bathtub, dried her feet and thrust them into a pair of sheepskin slippers. Her face was haphazardly made up, as if before a clouded mirror, with too much rouge, pencilled eyebrows not quite matching her own, cherry red lipstick and quantities of pinkish powder. To anyone with poor eyesight the effect was not displeasing, but gave her face a look of careless gaiety. She did her hair up in pins every night.

"There's a letter for you on the bookcase, Homer," she said, following him into the living room. She had been all for opening the letter the minute it arrived that morning, but Dolly had said, no, it would be unfair to Homer. Mrs. Bigelow had then suggested steaming the flap open and sealing it up again. Dolly had jibbed at that, too, so Mrs. Bigelow had gone downtown to escape temptation. But she had already, in imagination, bought herself one of those painting sets that come in a box; for surely Homer would have the decency to share his good fortune with her.

Homer switched on the television set and sat down to read his newspaper.

"Aren't you going to read your letter, Homer?" his mother-in-law asked.

"I have read it."

"You might have told me." Mrs. Bigelow spoke with more indignation than the occasion called for.

Since she was forced to accept charity from Dolly's husband, she naturally resented him at times. She accepted nothing from Grace's husband—in fact, she sometimes dipped into her own small hoard of pennies to buy him a package of the specially blended cigarettes he liked—and so he was her favorite. Like herself, Raymond was forced to live in circumstances quite unsuited to his nature. His parents had been well-to-do, had given him every advantage of education and upbringing. A person could tell at a glance that he possessed good breeding. Homer, on the other hand, constantly advertised to the world, by speech and action, his common upbringing. It was not poor Raymond's fault that his father had died bankrupt, nor was it Mrs. Bigelow's fault that after living in what she had considered at the time to be practically the lap of luxury—she had owned a grand piano, two oriental rugs, and a real oil painting that cost five hundred dollars, among other things—she had one day found herself penniless.

Once she had hoped to be an actress. In her younger days she had gone to New York with high hopes, but had never gotten farther than the chorus line in a musical comedy. Instead of going on from this to a great theatrical career, she had married a rich young man whose riches, it turned out later, were not the substantial kind inherited from wealthy parents. His financial position was not solid at all. It depended entirely on his ability to pick winning horses at the races. Mrs. Bigelow did not realize this at first. She lived like a duchess and gave no thought to where the money came from, until she found herself suddenly left alone in the world with two growing girls to feed, clothe and educate, and not a penny in the bank, not a cent of insurance even. She might have forgiven her husband for dying, but could not forgive him for leaving his widow destitute. She sold the piano, the rugs, the oil painting, and everything else she possessed, returned to her home city and took a job in a lingerie shop.

She had looked forward to the day when her daughters would marry and offer her the sanctuary of their homes. "From the time Dolly was a tiny baby, I'd counted on her marrying a man who could support us in style," she told her friends nowadays, "and look what she's got. An underpaid bank clerk. I never expected to end my days in a squalid little flat over a tobacco shop."

Homer, the giver of charity—such as it was—regarded his mother-in-law with that kindly protectiveness which all philanthropists feel for those whom they help. He thought she was becoming slightly addle-pated with advancing years, but he tolerated her eccentricities and was endlessly patient. "Second childhood," he told Dolly. "We all come to it, sooner or later." Mrs. Bigelow slept in the pull-down bed in the living room, and being often troubled with insomnia, wandered about the room in the dark, bumping into furniture, sometimes even picking out a tune on the mandolin. Dolly and Homer never complained about these disturbances, for they were both tender-hearted.

"You may read the letter if you like, Mother," Homer said kindly.

She was already reading it. "It's from those lawyers. They want you to go and see them. Dolly, those lawyers want Homer to go and see them about his aunt's estate."

"He's going tomorrow," Dolly said. She was setting the table in the small dining alcove.

"Well, I don't suppose he'll get more than a few hundred dollars," Mrs. Bigelow spoke disparagingly. "That old house of hers was ready for the wreckers, and *she* never looked as if she had two cents. That time I went to see her—out of the kindness of my heart—I didn't get a thing to eat but buttered bread."

"Every little bit helps," Dolly said, speaking of money.

"Especially when you're a pauper to begin with," her mother agreed, with a glance at Homer. He slapped a section of the newspaper against his knee to fold it, threw it aside and picked up another section.

"I wouldn't turn up my nose if it was five thousand," Dolly said.

"A piddling sum. . . . I do like the way you scruff up the newspaper so a person can't tell which page is which," Mrs. Bigelow told Homer, smoothing out the part he had thrown aside. "It shows great consideration."

"Dinner is ready," Dolly announced.

Homer turned up the sound on the television, for a Western was beginning. While they ate, the sound of pistol shots and of hoofs echoing down a canyon filled the room. They glanced from their plates to the screen and back again, not speaking.

After dinner. Mrs. Bigelow said, "When you've come into your immense fortune, Homer, perhaps you'd be interested in a business proposition." They were now watching a play in which the husband was arranging to do away with his wife by means of a pill containing deadly poison dropped into her whiskey glass.

Mrs. Bigelow raised her voice. "Perhaps you'd loan me fifty dollars."

"What for?" Homer took his eyes off the screen for a moment.

"To go into business."

Homer exchanged a look with his wife, then turned back to the play.

"You may laugh. I wouldn't expect *you* to see opportunity knocking if it came up and hit you in the face, but if we had fifty dollars, we could start a nice little business right here and make a fortune overnight.

"Who is 'we'?"

"Dolly and I."

"What is this new scheme?" Homer asked his wife. The commercial had come on and there was no danger of missing anything for the moment. "Making Granny's Gherkins?"

"Titter away! We could have made a success of that if you hadn't complained about the smell getting in your clothes. I haven't told Dolly about this one yet," Mrs. Bigelow confessed, "but naturally, since it is her home. . . . It's Granny's Greaseless Donuts," she said rather defiantly. "The machine costs fifty dollars. We'll sell them in all the shops."

Dolly wrinkled her forehead doubtfully. "Donuts would smell up the house worse than pickles, wouldn't they?"

"We can make up a batch every morning and air the place out afterwards. Do you want to hear some testimonials from people who have bought the machine? Listen. . . ." Mrs. Bigelow opened a brown manila envelope. " 'I paid for my machine the first week with Daisy's Donuts. I now have more orders than I can handle. Signed, Mrs. Daisy Thomas.' Mrs. Thomas calls hers Daisy's Donuts," she explained unnecessarily, in a bright voice, searching in vain for a spark of interest in the faces of her daughter and son-in-law.

The television story began again. "There's the glass with the poison in it," Homer said. "She's going to drink it."

Mrs. Bigelow glanced at the screen and saw that the heroine was indeed drinking from the glass containing the poison. The music rose to a crescendo. "Are you content to be a pauper for the rest of your life?" she shouted over it. "Have you no ambition? I will pay back the fifty dollars, of course," she added, lowering her voice as the music stopped. "With interest."

"We'll see, Mother," Homer said in a placating voice, but she knew he had no intention of seeing.

"I will try the bank," she said, refusing to admit defeat. "They won't pass up a chance to loan money on a sure thing. . . . And when I'm rich, I'll buy a television set that a person can *see*," she muttered, lapsing into offended silence. "I could buy the machine on time," she suggested after an interval. "Ten dollars down and the rest in easy instalments."

14

"We'll think about it, Mother," Dolly said.

"Think about it? I've *done* all the thinking, I'm not a complete fool, you know." She began to sulk. Nobody was paying the slightest attention to her. I might be a stick of furniture, she thought.

You're a fine-looking specimen, I must say, she went on to herself, staring at Homer's profile. I never thought, when I went to all the trouble of bringing Dolly into the world, seeing she was brought up properly, that she'd end up like this, in a tenement.

Homer had begun to doze. His head fell sideways against the back of his chair, and his mouth dropped open. His white jersey had shrunk in the wash and was stretched tight against his concave chest and rounded abdomen. "Oh, you are a handsome Harry!" Mrs. Bigelow said silently, her mouth curling with disdain.

Since nobody was paying any attention to her here, she decided to go across the hall to visit Grace.

With her own salary, plus her husband's pension, Grace managed so well that people marvelled, and held her up as an example of bravery in the face of misfortune. As soon as it became apparent that Raymond was unable to support her, she had shown great initiative in going to work as a receptionist in an advertising agency. Dressed in modish dark suits, her hair sleekly brushed and shaped, she sat behind a mahogany desk and made the proper impression on clients. At night she did her housework, pressed her clothes, and prepared Raymond's lunch for the following day. All this activity appeared more praise-worthy than it really was—especially to her mother—because Grace, younger than Dolly by ten years, had always been the spoiled one of the family, the pretty one. In temperament, too, she was quite unlike Dolly, who was plump and placid and made no attempt to fight off middle age. Grace fought the advancing years quite successfully. She dieted, was never too busy to make up her face properly, and spent ten minutes every night lubricating her skin with an expensive oil guaranteed to prevent wrinkles. As a result, she looked years younger than her age.

Raymond's lean fairness, his look and bearing of an underfed poet, made a perfect complement to Grace's dark good looks. Mrs. Bigelow still thought of them as children, two unfortunate children whom the fates had treated unkindly. Poor Raymond with his artificial foot and invalidish air, poor Grace, overworked, sometimes fretful, striving to keep up appearances. She would have given anything to help them. If Homer only had enough get-up-and-go to earn a decent living, she often thought. But Homer's salary was barely enough to feed himself.

Raymond had eaten dinner reclining on the couch, and now lay back with his hands behind his head, one elbow resting against his cleaned-up plate on the coffee table. Bleached furniture and pastel cotton rugs gave the flat a falsely modern appearance.

When Mrs. Bigelow asked him how he was he said, "Oh, God!" and rolled his eyes eloquently upward.

"You poor thing, you! Is it your back again?"

"I haven't been able to move off this couch all day." Raymond turned and rested on one elbow, grimacing to show how much this slight movement pained him. "I've had this excruciating headache, too." He closed his eyes, but opened them again when Grace poured coffee and set a plate of cakes on the table beside him.

Mrs. Bigelow immediately reproached herself for not having dropped in to see him during the day. Usually, he spent every afternoon in the reading room of the public library, going through the help-wanted ads in the newspapers.

"Get yourself a cup from the sideboard, will you, Mother? I'm too tired to move." Grace sat down with a long sigh and kicked off her shoes. Her figure, though trim, was not slim. Her feet ached constantly.

The cups were thick and shallow, all one color, quite unlike the fragile flowered china Mrs. Bigelow had used when she was a young wife. "All this work is wearing you out," she said as she helped herself to coffee.

"Somebody must feed and clothe us." At the sudden pained expression on Raymond's face, Grace looked aside.

"Did you know that Homer got a letter from those lawyers about his aunt's estate? He's going to see them tomorrow."

"Well, I hope he gets something out of it." Raymond looked pessimistic. "It's about time somebody around here had a little luck."

"You haven't found a job yet, you poor thing?"

Raymond recoiled as if wounded. "I haven't even got the strength to *look* for one."

"Can't the doctor do anything?"

"Oh, the doctor! I think I'm beyond all doctors."

"Dr. Phipps said there wasn't a thing the matter with him," Grace said.

"That old quack!" Raymond lay back, groaning. "What does he know?"

"You might try getting up off that damned couch, as he suggested," Grace snapped. She squeezed her feet back into her shoes and went into the kitchen.

"That's the kind of sympathy I get," Raymond said sadly.

Sensing tension in the air, Mrs. Bigelow finished her

coffee quickly and went home, where she spent the evening reading a book entitled, *One Thousand and One Ways to Make Money*.

In his dreams, Homer escaped to a brighter world, not exactly the world as it had been thirty years ago, for everyone was worse off then, but to a state of mind he had enjoyed then, when he was still young and full of hope, confident that next year, or the year after, things would begin to come his way. He would be promoted to office manager, or he would get a job with a company which appreciated his talents, and would climb rapidly to the top. Awake, he remembered too many lost opportunities, turns that he might have taken and had not. The years had slipped by so stealthily. It was not until he was nearing fifty that he suddenly realized he was hopelessly behind everyone else in the race toward success. He met old acquaintances, men he had worked with years before, men whom he had considered quite ordinary, not a bit smarter than he was, and learned that they had become vice-presidents of corporations, or had gone into business for themselves and made a fortune. All this had happened overnight, it seemed to him, while his back was turned. At first he tried to make excuses. Of course George (or Harry, or Dick) makes a lot of money, he told himself when he met one of these successful men, but he's probably got ulcers. He has overtaxed his strength and will drop dead of a heart attack before he can enjoy his wealth. He has worked so hard to get where he is that he has never found time to *live*. But these excuses offered small comfort, for Homer had worked hard, too, and worried a great deal, his indigestion could develop into ulcers overnight, and lately he had begun to suspect that his heart was weak. And had he ever found time to really enjoy life? No, I can't make excuses, he thought. Why not admit that luck's been against me? When he met the Georges, fat with success, glowing with confidence and good will, he felt depressed for days. In the night he could almost hear time running by, leaving him behind. He awoke every morning to dread—not a dread of something happening, but of something *not* happening; of having to continue forever in the same rut.

He had two hobbies. One was reading detective stories. He not only read them, he studied the plot and structure of each one, sometimes beginning with the last chapter so as to determine what methods the writer had employed in throwing the reader off the scent of the real criminal. For long he had cherished an ambition to write mystery novels himself, and several times had even gone so far as to purchase a notebook at the five and ten. But when he opened the notebook and saw the virgin pages, he felt that he was not quite ready to begin writing. He must wait for the knack to come to him, which it would do, he believed, like a revelation, between one day and the next. To start before the revelation came to him would be to invite failure.

His other hobby was reading seed catalogs and gardening guides. The only garden he had ever owned was in a box outside the kitchen window, but one day he hoped to have a real garden where he could grow everything—flowers, fruits, vegetables. He looked forward to this day with great longing.

Since the death of his aunt, he had felt justified in hoping that both his dreams might be realized when he retired. He thought of a small house in the country, and himself puttering in the garden—where it was always full summer—or writing his detective stories beside an open window with a view of cut hedges and flowers in

sunshine; once a month walking to the village post
office to pick up his retirement check.

Dolly telephoned Homer's office the next afternoon. He
was not there, the girl said; in fact, he had not been seen
all day.

"No doubt he's spending his immense fortune," Mrs.
Bigelow remarked. "Buying a yacht, perhaps." When she
had finished laughing she went on polishing the knives,
for she made herself useful about the house in little ways.

"I don't see why you think it's so funny, Homer coming into a little money," Dolly complained.

"You have no sense of humor," her mother said,
throwing down one knife and picking up another.
Sometimes she wondered if Dolly were lacking in
common sense as well. A woman who was blind to
Homer's shortcomings, who considered him more than
adequate as a husband and a provider, must be lacking in
something.

When six o'clock came, and Homer had not arrived,
Dolly began to worry. "I hope he hasn't done anything
foolish," she said.

"Such as . . . ?"

"He might think he should buy me a present, and
spend too much on it."

"A mink coat, perhaps?"

Mrs. Bigelow was still chuckling at this witticism
when Homer's key was heard in the lock. "Ah, the
millionaire!" she cried, as soon as he opened the door.
"Well, you haven't changed a bit, Homer. Money hasn't
spoiled you, I see."

Homer dropped some parcels on the table and kissed
his wife. This ritual was one that never failed to annoy his
mother-in-law. "Slobbering over one another morning

and evening," she said once to Dolly. "Your father wouldn't have *dared*."

"What are these?" she asked, when the kissing was over.

"Presents. One for each of you. Oh, and a bottle of champagne," Homer added carelessly. "I thought we should celebrate."

"Is everything settled, then," Dolly asked. "Did you get the money?"

Homer nodded, not looking at her.

It was less than he expected, Dolly thought.

"Perfume." Mrs. Bigelow opened one of the parcels. "Never mind, perhaps I can find a use for it."

"One is rose and the other lilac," Homer explained. "I thought you could decide which one will take which. It was the only thing I could think of," he added, noticing his mother-in-law's expression.

"I appreciate your sentiments, Homer, but really, you shouldn't have spent your entire fortune on us. We would have been grateful for some *little* thing."

"But what did the lawyers say?" Dolly asked.

"I'll tell you at dinner. I want to change now. I've had rather a busy day." Homer wore an expression of such arranged composure that Dolly supposed he had bought the perfume and the champagne in a pitiful attempt to make light of his disappointment.

"I'll take the rose, Dolly, if you don't mind. The lilac smells like a funeral. Champagne." Mrs. Bigelow opened the last parcel and held the bottle up to read the label. "What are we having for dinner?"

"Ham hocks."

"Perfect! Ham hocks and champagne. We might be entertaining the Queen of England."

"I thought of cooking something special, then I

thought, what if Aunt Harriet left us nothing, there would
be no reason to celebrate and it would only make it seem
worse." Dolly took the seldom-used wineglasses from the
cupboard and dusted them. "Oh, and a bowl of ice," she
said over her shoulder. "Champagne should be served
chilled."

"Chilled by all means," her mother agreed. "I'll speak
to the butler." Before Dolly had finished hacking ice
cubes out of the tray, she had found a corkscrew. The
cork came out of the bottle with a satisfying explosion,
and the champagne bubbled over the top and down
the sides. To save it, Mrs. Bigelow poured a glass and
drank it.

"All dressed up for the party, I see," she greeted Homer
gaily when he came from the bedroom wearing his
comfortable jersey. Dolly had found a pair of red candles
left over from Christmas and these, in brass holders,
decorated the center of the table. "Notice the feast we
have spread in your honor," Mrs. Bigelow told him as
Dolly came in with the plates. "You won't get a meal
like this at the Ritz." When he had filled her glass—first
glancing at the lowered contents of the bottle, then at
Dolly, but saying nothing—she held it up in a celebrating
gesture before she drank. "Now you must tell us all
about your adventures, Homer," she said kindly.

"I can't eat a thing," Dolly said. "How much *did* Aunt
Harriet leave you, Homer?"

But Homer would not divulge this information; not
until they had each drunk two glasses of champagne.
Dolly did not enjoy hers, but Mrs. Bigelow felt more
confident. She remembered the time Homer had got a
raise at the office, years and years ago. He had come home
with such a long face that they wondered what misfortune had befallen him. It was not until an hour after

dinner that he sprang his surprise. Before that—so he said afterwards—he had twice gone into the bedroom to have a good laugh by himself, imagining what they would say when they heard the good news. When he did get around to telling them, it fell flat, of course. Their joy was tinged with resentment at having been made to wait so long. A man getting a raise ought to come home with his arms full of flowers, and announce the news in ringing tones, then his womenfolk would know how to act. Of course Homer's raise had been a very small one, hardly a surprise at all.

"I telephoned the office," Dolly said at last. "They said you hadn't been in."

"I did drop in later, around five." Homer helped himself to another piece of pie.

"I hope they didn't mind your taking the day off."

"As a matter of fact, old Harris was pretty peeved. 'Who do you think you are?' he said to me. 'Walking in here ten minutes before closing time.' I told him to go to hell." Homer picked up his glass and took a casual sip. "You don't believe me, I see. My exact words, as near as I can remember, were, 'Go to hell, you old jackass,' or words to that effect."

"You're drunk," Mrs. Bigelow observed, but she gave Homer a sharp glance. It was just conceivable that he *had* spoken to Mr. Harris in that way. Once in a great while—oh, at very rare intervals—he did stand up on his hind legs and assert himself, usually with disastrous results. Like the time he had knocked Mr. Williams, a former landlord, downstairs. "Some people get drunk on a thimbleful," she added.

"I'm sober as a judge."

"He would have fired you," Dolly said.

"As a matter of fact, he did."

"Don't joke, Homer. It's too frightening."

"You'd be laughing on the other side of your face if he had," Mrs. Bigelow said. "You're acting very peculiar," she decided. "Has your immense fortune gone to your head? It'll be a different story when you have to face Mr. Harris tomorrow morning."

"I won't *be* facing him."

"Homer . . . !" Dolly was beginning to panic. "You haven't really lost your job?"

"Well, he threatened to fire me, so I quit."

Dolly covered her eyes. Sometimes in the darkest part of the night she woke up thinking, what if Homer lost his job? This was about the worst thing she could imagine happening, for she belonged to the generation that feared unemployment.

"You blockhead!" Mrs. Bigelow shouted louder than she meant to. She was a little drunk herself. "So you've lost your job. And what are we going to live on, might I ask? I didn't bring up my daughter to starve in a gutter."

"It's all right, Dolly. I didn't mean to frighten you." Homer tried to put his arms around his wife, but Mrs. Bigelow pushed herself between them.

"Oh, no, he didn't mean to frighten us. Faced with starvation in our declining years—that shouldn't frighten anyone."

"We've got Aunt Harriet's money, Dolly. I was only having a bit of fun with you. I never thought you'd get upset."

"Fun!" Mrs. Bigelow gave him another push. "I like your idea of fun."

Dolly took her hands from her face. "You shouldn't joke about things like that, Homer—about losing your job. Supposing it came true?"

"But it has come true!" Homer shouted to drown out

his mother-in-law. "I don't *need* a job, Dolly. Aunt Harriet's left us a fortune."

Dolly stared at him. "You're joking again," she said in a frightened voice.

"No, I'm not. I've been laughing to myself, thinking of the looks on your faces when I told you."

"How much . . . ?" Dolly shrank back into her chair as if she dreaded his answer.

"Two hundred and fifty thousand," Homer said calmly. "A quarter of a million."

"Ha, ha!" Mrs. Bigelow exclaimed with withering sarcasm.

"It was more than that, really," Homer went on. "That's what we'll have left after we pay the taxes and the death duties and everything. And the house, too."

"You're not serious," Mrs. Bigelow said. "That champagne has gone to your head."

"I am serious."

"You mean to sit there and tell us that your Aunt Harriet actually left you two hundred and fifty thousand dollars?"

"Yes."

"I don't believe it."

"You can believe it or not. It's true."

Dolly's face crumpled suddenly. "Why on earth didn't you tell us when you came in?" she cried in a furious voice. To steady herself she picked up her glass to drink, but her hand trembled so that the champagne slopped on the white tablecloth.

"I've been laughing to myself all through dinner. I had a good laugh in the bedroom while I was changing."

"Sitting there all through dinner, letting us think you hadn't even got as much as you expected . . . !" Dolly burst into tears. "And saying that about losing your job!" She groped for a corner of the tablecloth to wipe her eyes.

"Oh, now look, Dolly, don't *cry*!" Homer dabbed at her cheek with a crumpled paper napkin. "I thought you'd be glad."

"I just don't know what to *think*!" Dolly wept.

"Where did your Aunt Harriet ever get two hundred and fifty thousand dollars?" Mrs. Bigelow demanded.

"Lift up your head, Dolly. There's no sense crying."

"I wouldn't know how to *spend* that much money!" Dolly raised her head, but the tears still fell.

"She never made that kind of money running a boarding house. Was it in the bank, or what?"

"In stocks, and real estate. I don't care how she made it. All I'm interested in is how we'll spend it."

"I always thought there was something funny about those boarders of hers. Her young ladies, she used to call them. 'What do they do?' I asked her, that time I went to see her. 'They're secretaries,'' she said. 'Then why are they at home today?' I asked. 'It's their day off,' she told me. In the middle of the week."

"Mother, what are you saying?" Dolly stopped crying to listen.

"I'm saying about Homer's aunt; how she made her money."

"She made it in real estate," Homer said.

"I wasn't born yesterday. I'm not a babe in the woods. I know all about Lavinia Street. So now it will be your house, Homer. You'll be running it. Well, it will be a change from the bank, I'll say that."

"We're selling the house."

"Why sell it? If your aunt made that much money, why kill the golden goose?"

"Oh, Mother . . . !"

"I wouldn't go jumping to conclusions," Homer warned. "Just because Aunt Harriet happened to live on Lavinia Street. . . . She was a perfectly respectable woman and you know it."

"I'm not jumping. I've known all along." Mrs. Bigelow already believed that she had entertained suspicions about Harriet Jeffries for some time. Then, belatedly, she realized that Homer's voice had taken on a new note of authority. She realized also that he was no longer a penniless bank clerk, but a man of property who might resent aspersions being cast at his aunt. "Perhaps I was jumping to conclusions," she agreed. "I apologize." Owning herself in the wrong was so new to her that she looked sheepish.

"But where did she get the money?" Dolly wanted to know.

Homer shrugged. "Playing the stock market. Speculating in real estate."

"Why didn't she ever spend any of it on herself? She could have gone to Florida every winter. She didn't own a car, even."

"She liked making money, not spending it."

"Lucky for us," Mrs. Bigelow said. "We're millionaires!" she cried. "We'll be hobnobbing with the Vanderbilts. We'll blossom out in mink coats, Dolly. We'll take a trip around the world."

"Hold on, now!" Homer threw cold water on these plans, but he laughed happily. "I might have something to say about how we spend this money."

Mrs. Bigelow gave him a good stare. Selfish, as usual. But she brightened after a moment and said, "Well, I know one thing, you could knock me over with a feather this minute." She picked up the bottle and was about to polish off the remainder of the champagne, then changed

27

her mind. Homer was in control of the money, as he had so rudely pointed out, and her position demanded that she curry favor. "Why don't you finish this, Homer?" She forced a smile as she filled his glass.

"I don't mind if I do." He sat back and flung one knee over the other, feeling expansive, kindly, dominating his surroundings, a man of distinction.

"I'll break the news to Grace." Mrs. Bigelow made her way in an uneven line toward the door. The carpet went up and down, giving her a lovely sensation like being on a gentle roller coaster.

Behind her Dolly said again in a bewildered voice, "I just don't know what to *think*!"

Chapter Two

HOMER had been handling other people's money all his adult life, and knew the value of it. He spent nothing recklessly. He bought a good second-hand car—a black sedan—and a house. The remainder of his legacy—including the money received from the sale of the house on Lavinia Street; it had fetched a price that staggered him—he placed in the care of the firm that had handled his aunt's investments.

His mother-in-law, when she learned that his income would not support a villa in the south of France and a house at Palm Beach, advised a different course of action.

"You must go into business, Homer," she said. "Buy a nice gift shop, or a restaurant."

"Or a donut factory?"

"I fail to see the joke. What will you do then, get another job?" She was tired of having him underfoot all day.

"No, I think not."

"But surely you don't intend to sit around doing nothing for the rest of your life?"

"That's exactly what I do intend."

"And live on the piddling income from your aunt's money?" She was adjusting rapidly. What she now called

a piddling income she would once have considered more
than enough to support a family in luxury.

"My needs are not great," Homer said.

"But what will you *do* with yourself?"

"I have plans."

Homer and Dolly spent a month looking for a house.
They decided at last on an eight-roomed cottage an
hour's drive from the city. They both knew, the minute
they saw it, that it was the house for them. Slant-roofed,
with rosy chimneys, it was set in two acres of lovely old
trees and sloping lawns. Neighboring houses were
screened from view by tall hedges. Even in late March,
with patches of stale snow under the evergreens and
nothing showing in the flower beds but green spears of
tulips and daffodils, the garden was beautiful. English
violets grew in corners, and a little pool, drained for the
winter months, was edged with rocks where crocuses
and blue myrtle grew. There was a stone garage with a
great weeping willow hanging over it. And, hidden
away at the back, behind a cedar hedge, was a small
gardener's cottage. Flagged walks led to rose arbors and
to shaded nooks that later would be filled with wild-
flowers.

This place was called Dove Cottage; a beautiful name,
Dolly thought, promising happiness and tranquility.

Homer recognized the interior of the house at once. It
was straight out of an Agatha Christie novel. There was
the stone hearth, its polished brass fenders reflecting the
light from the leaded windows, the wide stairway with
its landing halfway up—the very spot for a body to be
found. In the study, down the hall from the living room,
french doors led to a garden terrace. (He saw himself
sitting at a desk in the study, facing the sunny windows,
surrounded by books, writing his mystery stories.) The

casement windows in the dining room opened onto another view of the garden. Upstairs were four oddly-shaped bedrooms and a chipped bath.

"You could scarcely call it modern," Mrs. Bigelow remarked. "That kitchen came out of the ark." If Homer had taken her advice about going into business, they could have a many-roomed mansion with half a dozen servants.

"It needs fixing up," Homer admitted. "The whole house needs redecorating. We could remodel the kitchen, and put in another bath. . . . Could you be happy here, Dolly?"

"Oh, *yes!*" Dolly cried. "It's the sort of house I've always wanted."

"Then we'll buy it."

"I expect the roof leaks," Mrs. Bigelow said.

"Why couldn't we fix up the gardener's cottage for Raymond and Grace?" Homer was speaking to Dolly. "We could invite them out for the summer. Grace hasn't been looking at all well since she had that bout of flu. Perhaps if she gave up her job for the summer, and they moved out here, Raymond might get back on his feet again, too."

"Mr. Moneybags dispensing charity," his mother-in-law muttered under her breath. She was really giving vent to her disappointment about the house, for she had hoped that Homer would buy a place in the city or, better, rent the largest suite in an ultra-modern apartment building.

She had to admit, later on, that redecorating all the rooms vastly improved the interior of the house. The kitchen was remodeled, after a fashion. That is, some new cabinets were installed, as well as all the latest in electrical appliances. Homer decided that further improvements, such as the extra bath and a new heating system, could wait until later on. They moved to Dove Cottage in mid-April.

Given a choice of bedrooms, Mrs. Bigelow chose a small corner room from which she could watch the road, though she saw nothing going by, the first day, except a group of village children on their way to school. She had never lived in the country, and was certain she would not like it. The first night she could not sleep, everything was so quiet. She heard nothing but a dog barking now and then in the distance. But in the morning—in the middle of the night, really, before the sun was fully up—a red bird sat on the lombardy poplar outside her window and whistled loud enough to deafen her. Then robins sang, and a pair of doves tossed mournful messages back and forth.

"Why don't you go away and let me sleep?" She opened the window and stuck her head out, flapping a towel. The red bird flew away, but came back and whistled louder than ever the minute she withdrew her head. She closed the window and covered her head with a blanket.

She was dropping off to sleep again when she heard Homer stoking the furnace in the cellar. Clank, clank, went the radiator. We might as well be living in pre-historic times, she thought. Imagine a coal furnace, in this day and age. We're hardly any better off than we were before we got the money. If Homer had gone into business as I suggested, or even taken a job, instead of trying to live on his income, we might enjoy a few comforts. But, no, he had to give up his job and live like a country gentleman, hanging around the house all day, getting in everyone's way.

She felt better when she threw off the blankets and saw the sun on her new furniture. It was something to have a room of one's own, with a blue rug on the floor and full-length curtains of flowered chintz at the windows. She rose and took from the closet her new painting outfit: a box for carrying her paints, brushes and palette, a portable aluminum easel, a folding stool, and ten beautiful untouched canvas panels. Today she meant to begin her first painting.

After breakfast Homer drove to the village. Dolly was still fussing with her new furniture, trying chairs in various positions, shifting tables, polishing her new piano. Every few minutes she sat down and picked out a tune that had been popular when she was young: "Tiptoe Through the Tulips" or "Rose Marie." Her touch was unsure. Once, long ago, she had played the piano very nicely, but of course she had got out of practice, not having had one for so many years. "You're getting the hang of it," her mother encouraged. "With a little practice you'll be as good as ever. We'll have some nice duets. See if you can remember 'Mississippi Mud.' That's a good one for the mandolin."

"Are you going painting, Mother?"

"I don't know what to paint," Mrs. Bigelow confessed. "I don't see a thing that appeals to me. If we were in the city I'd go to the park and paint the duck pond, but since we're stuck out here in the country, at the end of nowhere . . ."

"You could do the weeping willow beside the garage."

"You want something more than a bare tree in a picture. I'm going for a walk. Perhaps I'll see a nice view."

"If you're going to the village, there's a short-cut through the fields."

Mrs. Bigelow went outside and tested the air. It was a fine warm day with flying clouds. A handful of daffodils bloomed in a sheltered spot beside the driveway. The

c 33

village, hidden from view, lay beyond some upward-sloping fields. She found the short-cut, a narrow path running beside a fence, and ventured rather timidly along it. There might be cattle in the field. She didn't fancy being chased by an enraged bull. The path was wet and slippery. She skirted around puddles, keeping her eyes open for a view, seeing nothing that would make a nice picture until she passed a screen of low evergreens marking the boundaries of a neglected cemetery. Then, there lay the village in a shallow valley, with hills going up behind it and fluffy clouds above it; white houses, church spires, red barns, smoke from chimneys—everything needed to make a painting.

There was nowhere to sit near the path, so she wandered a little way into the cemetery and rested on a lichened stone while she contemplated the scene. A portly man in a youthfully checkered hat and a plaid sports jacket puffed up the path from the village. He stopped when he saw her, then picked his way toward her.

"I beg your pardon." He removed his hat momentarily, showing a glimpse of polished bald head. "Are you by any chance the new owner of Dove Cottage?"

Mrs. Bigelow looked him up and down. "I'm not the owner, exactly, but I live there."

His face broke into a smile. "I saw you were a stranger, so I said to myself, 'She must be our new neighbor.' I thought I'd better introduce myself. I'm George Adams. I live two houses down the road."

Mrs. Bigelow nodded with cool politeness. She was not accustomed to carrying on conversations with perfect strangers.

George Adams took off his hat again and fanned himself with it. His forehead shone with perspiration. "I live with my son and daughter-in-law."

Mrs. Bigelow softened a little. Here was another poor soul forced to put up with relatives. "I hope they treat you properly," she said before she thought.

"Oh, yes, they treat me well enough. Why shouldn't they? I own the house. Besides, I'm not hard to live with. I'm not one of these old stick-in-the-muds. I have hobbies. I keep young." He brushed some last year's leaves from a headstone and sat down. "You'd never think I was seventy, now, would you?" He beamed at her, inviting inspection. His face was round and shiny as an apple. His eyes, behind steel-rimmed spectacles, were blue.

"You look more like sixty to me."

"That's what everybody says. They say, 'George, you don't look a day over sixty.' Well, I was seventy my last birthday."

"I'd never believe it."

"Is your husband living?" he asked.

"My husband?" Mrs. Bigelow had almost forgotten she ever had one. "Oh, he's dead. He died years ago. I live with my daughter."

"It's a wonder a good-looking woman like you hasn't married again."

Why, the old flirt! Mrs. Bigelow thought, highly pleased. "I never saw a man I liked well enough," she said tartly.

"I bet you turned down a good dozen. Are you interested in hobbies, by any chance?"

"I paint," Mrs. Bigelow said, with a glance at the landscape.

"Pictures, do you mean?" His eyes brightened with admiration. "I never tried anything like that. I don't suppose I'd have the knack. Do you need any special training?"

"Grandma Moses never had any training. She just sat down and started to paint."

"Is that how you began—just sat down and painted a picture?"

"Well . . . yes." It was how she was going to begin, at any rate.

"If somebody gave me a few pointers, I might try it myself," he said hopefully. She made no comment. "Well, I must be off," he said. "I don't suppose you'd mind if I dropped around one day to look at your paintings?"

She started, and searched her mind for an excuse. "I really haven't anything worth looking at."

"Oh, go on!"

"No, really. I haven't a thing I'd want to show anyone."

"You're just being modest. I know you painters—always criticizing your own work. I'll bet you've got some real masterpieces. I'm coming up to see them one of these days," he warned, shaking a playful finger at her.

"Perhaps later on I'll have something worth showing."

"Are you walking back?" He rose and offered his arm.

"Not just yet."

He replaced his checkered hat, which Mrs. Bigelow rather admired. From the path he called back, "Don't forget, now; I'm coming around to see those paintings!"

Back home, after his trip to the village, Homer hung his new rakes and shovels in the garage. He was ready to begin gardening, but he hesitated to disturb the soil in any of the beds before consulting with Mr. Newby, the combination odd-jobs man and gardener he had engaged that morning, for despite all the reading he had done, he was not certain whether the new shoots pushing up here and there were weeds or garden plants. He recognized tulips and irises, and the splayed leaves of delphiniums, but little else.

Every tiny plant filled him with delight, each unfolding bud seemed to him like a miracle about to happen, each bird-call echoed his own happiness. His old life seemed so far behind that he could almost believe he had never lived it.

In the village that morning, as he set up charge accounts in the shops and did his business at the bank, he realized that his attitude toward people—shopkeepers, bank employees and the like—was changing. He felt assured, even exacting, where formerly he would have exhibited diffidence. In the bank, where he had already opened an account, giving his occupation as "retired banker", he was waited on with a scurrying deference he recognized. It was the treatment he himself, in the old days, had reserved for very important customers.

He puttered around the garden all morning, accomplishing nothing, but enjoying every minute.

"This is the life, eh, Dolly?" he said, when she came out to tell him that lunch was ready. "See that red bird? That's a cardinal."

"Oh, isn't he pretty! I never saw one before."

"We'll get a bird book, so we can tell the different kinds. I've seen half a dozen this morning that I didn't recognize."

Mrs. Bigelow did not appear for lunch. "She's out painting," Dolly explained.

"She's never missed a meal before."

"She saw a nice view that she wanted to paint, so she came right home and got her things. She could hardly wait to begin her first picture. She took a packet of sandwiches and a thermos of coffee. She's in the old cemetery, near the short-cut to the village."

"I wonder why she took up painting. She doesn't know the first thing about it."

"She's got a book called *How to Paint a Landscape*. We mustn't discourage her, Homer. We mustn't say anything, no matter how badly her first picture turns out. It gives her something to do; keeps her happy. She always wanted to take up painting, you know, but could never afford the materials."

"I'm not going to discourage her. I like to see people happy. As a matter of fact, I think it's wonderful to see a woman your mother's age keep so interested in things."

After lunch Homer took a nap in the study. Dolly had bought a desk and placed it near the window. On the desk was a thick tablet of ruled paper that he had purchased that morning in the village. Very soon he meant to begin writing his mystery novels—for now, surely, when he had time to think, the revelation would come to him. He would set aside a certain number of hours each day, and these hours would be devoted to writing. Half sleeping, he dreamed that he was well launched on his project. He was seated at the desk, with sunshine flooding the room. Words flowed from his pen. On a shelf beside the desk was a whole row of books he had written. A folded newspaper bore a headline beginning, "Mr. Homer Flynn, the famous writer . . ."

He woke up so refreshed that he decided to quickly dispose of a number of unpleasant jobs that needed doing, such as cleaning out the cellar. The cellar was not the best part of the house. It was divided into three rooms, one a sort of workroom with a counter and a place to hang tools, another housing the hot-water heater and the laundry tubs, and a third which was the furnace room. He planned, later on, to replace the outmoded coal furnace with a modern oil burner, but that would have to wait until summer, when the fire could be let out. In the meantime, he faced every day the unpleasant job of banking the furnace and, worse, of taking out ashes. He did not know how to dispose of the ashes that he had already accumulated. He did not fancy dumping them in the garden. There appeared to be no service in the village for the removal of ashes.

The furnace room was under the study. It received light from two small windows set high up, and these windows were partially screened by shrubbery, so that the room was perpetually twilight. Two electric bulbs hung from the ceiling. The coal bin was in one corner. The ash tubs and hardwood logs for the fireplace were stacked neatly along one wall. But in the middle of the floor lay a great jumble of empty boxes, fruit baskets, old newspapers and other trash.

Faced with the problem of dealing with this accumulation of rubbish, Homer could think of nothing better than to stack it more neatly in a corner. Doing this, he came upon what he first took to be the cover of a heavy wooden packing box. Removing it with great effort— for it turned out to be constructed of solid two-by-fours —he uncovered a round hole, less than three feet across, in the concrete floor. He could not see the bottom of the hole. He went back upstairs, got a flashlight, and lowered it into the dark opening, discovering a dry well, narrow and very deep—so deep that he could just make out, in the dim glow from the flashlight, some rotting boards and broken crockery at the bottom.

"Come and take a look at this, Dolly," he called. "There's an old well down here. Now, why do you suppose anyone ever dug a well down here?"

"Don't fall in, for heaven's sake." Dolly peered timidly into the cavity. "Cover it up. It makes me nervous."

"I could throw the ashes from the furnace in here. I've been wondering what to do with them."

"Do get it filled up quickly, then, Homer. Somebody *could* fall in, you know. It frightens me to think of it."

"The body in the well," Homer said, and suddenly inspiration came to him. *The Body in the Well.* What a title for his first book! He peered down into the depths with morbid fascination. Perhaps there *was* a body down there.

"I can't bear to look at it," Dolly said with a shiver. "Put the cover back on, Homer."

"In a minute. You go on upstairs if you're nervous. I won't fall in."

"You're all covered with coal dust, too."

When Dolly had gone upstairs he lowered the flashlight on the string for another look. If there was anything out of the ordinary down there, it was well covered with debris. He was almost disappointed. For a moment he had hoped that there might really be a body down there, an old one, a nice clean skeleton, that would provide an intriguing mystery. He saw himself, with the help of the village police, unravelling bit by bit the fascinating story of—what? A beautiful young wife and her lover, both slain by the jealous husband? A rich elderly widow who had kept her money hidden behind a loose brick in the fireplace, done in by her favorite but treacherous nephew?

He decided not to fill the well with ashes just yet, for he was reluctant to give up the idea that there might be some mystery at the bottom. He replaced the cover and swept the floor, then went upstairs and took a shower. When he had finished cleaning up he went down to the study, where a cheerful fire was burning in the fireplace.

It was the quiet part of the day. Dolly was in the kitchen, from which drifted a smell of cooling pies and roasting meat. Outside, mourning doves were calling. The April afternoon had become overcast, and a thin mist obscured the distant landscape. The change in the weather made being inside by the fire more pleasant.

He sat down at the desk, pulled the lovely untouched thick white pad of paper towards him, turned back the cover and wrote, 'The Body in the Well, by Homer Flynn, page one,' and began casting about in his mind for a good opening sentence.

Mrs. Bigelow came in through the back door, making a great deal of noise. "All this paraphernalia," she grumbled, dragging her collapsible easel up the steps. The grumbling was simply a cover-up. She did not want to appear too eager to display the paint-laden canvas which she held gingerly by one corner. The rest of her painting equipment she carried in her other hand, or tucked under one arm. She had dropped the easel and the folding stool several times on the way home, but would not relinquish her grasp on the canvas, for she wanted nothing to happen to it.

Dolly opened the door and relieved her of the most cumbersome articles. "I'm dying to see your picture, Mother. Put it on the counter, so I can get a good look at it."

"It's just a landscape. . . . Mind you don't rub it. That paint's still wet."

"It's *lovely*, Mother!" Dolly cried.

"Oh, it's nothing much." Her mother tried to appear casual.

"But it will be when you've finished it. I think it's simply wonderful."

"Finished?" The nonchalant expression Mrs. Bigelow had arranged on her face dissolved into vexation. "It *is* finished."

"Of course. I can see that it is, now that I've had a good look at it."

"Did you think it wasn't finished?"

"I want Homer to see it. May I carry it into the study? We can hang it over the fireplace to dry. Homer," Dolly called out before she reached the study, "here's Mother's first picture, all finished!"

"Say . . . !" Homer took the canvas from her and placed it on the mantelpiece, then backed away, his head on one side like a connoisseur. "That's what I call a painting!"

"It's a landscape," Dolly said helpfully.

"And a very good one, too. You'd never know it wasn't done by a real professional."

"Dolly thought it wasn't finished."

"How could you think that, Dolly?" Homer turned to her reproachfully. "*I* knew it was finished the minute I saw it. Even to the name down in the corner," he added, noting this for the first time.

Mrs. Bigelow cast pleased smiles all around. "I thought it wasn't bad," she admitted.

"It's excellent. We must buy a frame for it tomorrow. I particularly like your cows," Homer added, still scrutinizing the picture, his mouth pursed in a considering way.

"Cows?" Mrs. Bigelow's face darkened.

Homer started, not quite sure whether he had blundered. "This red one. . . ." He pointed.

"That's a barn."

"Oh . . . ! And these white things . . . ?"

"They're houses, of course." Mrs. Bigelow moved forward to screen the painting from Homer's view, as if his examination had desecrated it. "Cows!" she said angrily. "I never saw a cow with smoke coming out of it before."

"Oh, *now* I can see that they're houses!" Homer exclaimed, stepping sideways to get a better view. "I couldn't really see, before, because of the light. Why, I recognize some of them!" He was trying his best to make amends, but now Mrs. Bigelow detected the false enthusiasm in his voice. "Your colors are lovely," he went on, overdoing it still further. "Such lovely green grass and blue sky!"

"Those are clouds in the sky, in case you don't recognize them. I suppose you thought they were sheep."

"Leave it there, Mother; don't take it away," Dolly begged, as her mother removed the picture from the mantelpiece. "*I* knew they were houses all along," she added placatingly. "It really is a beautiful painting, Mother. I want to frame it and hang it right there over the fireplace. It's just what this room needs."

Mrs. Bigelow hesitated, cast a suspicious glance at Homer, then decided, since she wanted to have another look at the picture herself, to place it back on the mantelpiece. He's jealous, she thought. That's what's the matter with him. He's jealous because *he* can't paint. He'd laugh on the other side of his face if it was hung in a museum. She saw the picture hanging in a large room. Crowds of people stared at it, and marvelled. "She didn't even *begin* painting until she was seventy-two," they were telling one another, "and now she's world-famous."

Her antagonism for Homer lasted all through dinner, and colored her evening reverie, when Homer, for some unknown reason, sat for three hours before his desk in the study drawing circles on a pad of paper, while she sat

43

with Dolly beside the fire in the living room. She imagined how it would be if she and Dolly were alone. When her husband was alive she had often daydreamed that he had met his end in various ways, so that when he did drop dead of a heart attack it was no shock to her, though his lack of insurance was. Now she pictured herself opening the door to a policeman, one of those handsome patrolmen she had seen riding motorcycles along the highway. His face was kind. "I'm most terribly sorry, ma'am, to be the bearer of sad tidings, but your son-in-law has just met with a nasty accident." After the funeral she would advise Dolly to sell the house and take a trip to the south of France.

"Are you crying, Mother?"

Mrs. Bigelow came out of her reverie. "I was thinking of something very sad," she said. And indeed, in her dream, having disposed of Homer, she *was* sad, and mourned for him; had even got to the point of telling people—through her tears—that he had been kind to her. "I feel better now." She wiped the mist from her eyes. "I think I'll make some tea."

"Homer," she called into the study. "Would you like a nice cup of tea?"

But when she awoke next morning she was still not quite ready to forgive Homer for thinking her nice houses were cows. She went downstairs early and began to prepare breakfast, for she was eager to dispose of the few chores she did around the house each morning and be off outdoors with her painting outfit. As soon as she had started the coffee she went into the study to admire her picture. Her glance fell on the desk, and Homer's literary effort.

"Did you know that Homer's writing a book, Dolly?" she asked when her daughter came downstairs. "He's only got the title done, so far. He's calling it *The Body in the Well*."

"No, I didn't know, but he's often said that he would like to write mystery stories some day. I suppose he got the idea from that old well in the cellar."

"What well?"

Dolly's explanation so intrigued Mrs. Bigelow that she went down to examine the well herself. When she climbed the stairs to the kitchen again, Homer was eating breakfast.

"I've been looking at your well, Homer. I didn't see any body in it."

"You didn't take the cover off?"

"I did. How else could I see inside? I haven't got eyes like Superman."

"I don't want you to go near that well again, Mother." Homer laid down his fork and looked at her as if he meant business. "I'm going to fill it up with ashes, but until I do I consider it extremely dangerous. I don't want you or Dolly going near it, you understand?"

Mrs. Bigelow's head went up. "Oh, my, aren't we the bossy one since we took up the literary life!"

"No, really, Mother, I mean it," Homer said firmly.

"Are you going painting today, Mother?" Dolly asked.

"If I can find another nice herd of cows." Mrs. Bigelow gave Homer a dark look.

She set off an hour later, taking the path to the village, but going on past the cemetery toward a group of farm buildings she had noticed the day before. She was going to try something entirely different today. She was going to fill up her whole canvas with nothing but a big red barn, just one corner of the white farmhouse showing, and the farm pond and some white ducks in the foreground. She set up her easel beside an old root fence and began to paint.

She became so·lost in her art that she failed to notice the passing of time, until a whistle blowing in the village reminded her that she was hungry. She moved her stool back a few yards so that she could criticize what she had done, and unwrapped her sandwiches. She did not see George Adams approaching until he was almost beside her.

"By golly, that's pretty good!" he said admiringly. "Is that what you call abstract painting?"

"I belong to the Impressionist school," Mrs. Bigelow said, quoting from her book.

"If that's Tanner's barn, you've got the color just right."

"I like a picture with a nice lot of red in it."

"Well, you've got plenty of red there. You know, when I saw you yesterday, I thought maybe you were one of these amateur painters, like a couple of my daughter-in-law's friends. She's got some of their stuff hanging in the living room—trees and little brooks. I like buildings in a picture."

"So do I."

"They can't paint buildings, is the reason they don't. You've got to study perspective, Lola says, to be able to do buildings."

Mrs. Bigelow had skipped the chapter on perspective in *How to Paint a Landscape*. "How true," she said.

"Of course some of the better painters ignore perspective altogether," George said with a glance at her picture, "but you've got to know about it so you can ignore it intelligently."

"Have a sandwich," Mrs. Bigelow said.

"You sure you've got plenty?" He sat down and took one. "Lola'll have a fit when I don't show up for lunch. She's probably got what she calls a nice little salad all ready for me—a dab of cream cheese on a lettuce leaf. She's trying to improve my figure—won't let me eat bread. What I always tell her is, I've been fat all my life."

"I've been eating bread for seventy years and it hasn't killed me yet. Have some coffee."

"Go on!" he said, accepting the cup she held out. "It'll be a good many years before you see seventy."

"My daughter's fifty."

"You must have been one of those child brides, then. You don't look a day over fifty yourself."

Mrs. Bigelow was so unused to flattery that she blushed.

"Can I sit here and watch you work?" he asked, when they had finished eating. "Or does it make you nervous having an audience? Say," he went on, not giving her time to answer, "if I got some paints and brushes, and one of those easel things, would you show me how to begin? Fred and Lola are always after me to take up new hobbies, but what I say is, what's the fun of doing things by yourself? If I lived in the city, it'd be different. They've got clubs and things for retired people."

"Don't you like the country?"

"Well, Fred and Lola wanted to move out. We've been here three years. I used to have a nice little business in the city. Wholesale fish. I made a pile of money. Fred didn't want the business—didn't want to get his clothes smelt up, he said—so I sold out, and we moved out here. What I really wanted was to live in one of those twenty-story apartment buildings in the city, where I'd be close to anything. But Lola thought living in the country was more stylish. Fred's an accountant. He drives to his office in the city every day."

"That's where I'd live, if I had my choice," Mrs. Bigelow said. "Right in the middle of the city, where you

47

can see something besides trees. But Homer wanted to have a garden; and Dolly's got no gumption. Yes Homer this, yes Homer that. If he was to suggest living in the Fiji Islands, she'd agree."

"You've got exactly the same problem I have," George said.

They pondered this, while Mrs. Bigelow brightened up the red on the sunlit side of her barn.

"I guess he could afford to live anywhere, with the money he's got," George commented after a time.

"Who, Homer? He'd have a lot more if he'd take my advice and go into business. But, no, he wants to be a country gentleman."

"Well, I can understand these big executives getting fed up with the hurly-burly," George said tolerantly. "Rush, rush, rush, all day long. Now, in my little business, I could take a day off when I felt like it. With a big executive like your son-in-law, it's different. You've got to be on the job every minute."

Mrs. Bigelow stopped painting. "Who told you all this about Homer?"

"Fellow in the hardware store this morning. He said, 'I hear you got a rich neighbor, George. Mr. Flynn, the retired banker.' I guess everybody in the village knows your son-in-law by now. They've kind of taken to him, because he don't act like a rich man trying to impress them. Got a huge fortune, but drives an ordinary car, bought an ordinary house—acts just like one of them. Country people appreciate that. Too many city people only pretending to be rich come out here and put on the dog—look down their noses at the natives."

"So he's a retired banker now."

"Well, isn't he?"

"I guess you could call it that. He had a piddling little

job in the city, a clerk in the bank, then his aunt died and left him some money. She ran a bawdy house down on Lavinia Street."

"Oh, go on!" George turned beet red.

"She left him the house, too. That big old place with the green shutters."

"I've *heard* about Lavinia Street," George said doubtfully. "I don't know any of the houses. Does he still own it?"

"No, he got rid of it as fast as he could. Oh, Homer's not that kind," Mrs. Bigelow, seeing that George was embarrassed, tried to reassure him. "*He* didn't run it. It was only his aunt."

"Well. . ." George brought out his handkerchief and mopped his face with it. "I'm not going to tell Lola," he decided. "She's such a bloody—excuse me—such a darned snob. She might think . . ."

"My daughter's a real nice girl—a lady in every way. She was brought up properly. She was barely acquainted with Homer's aunt."

"I can believe that."

"She was practically a perfect stranger to all of us."

"What difference does it make, anyway?" George was regaining his composure. "Everybody's got skeletons in their closets. I had an uncle once who was a bootlegger."

Mrs. Bigelow nodded. "As I said to Homer, who cares where money comes from, as long as it comes?"

"Say, I like you!" George tucked his handkerchief back into his breast pocket so that one corner of the colored border made a neat triangle. "There's not many honest people left in this world. Everybody's trying to be something else, like Fred not wanting me to tell people I was in the fish business. 'What's wrong with fish?'

I ask him. Sure, they smell. I came home every night for forty years smelling so bad people crossed the street when they saw me coming, but I made a darn sight more money than Fred's making, even if he does wear a clean white shirt and his best suit every day."

"People are funny," Mrs. Bigelow agreed. "Did I tell you I was on the stage once?"

"An actress?"

"Not exactly. I was in burlesque." This was untrue, but she had so often—to shock people and to make herself appear more interesting—embroidered her brief far-off career in the chorus with this fiction that she had almost come to believe it herself.

"You mean one of those strip-teasers?"

"They didn't have strip-teasers in those days. Besides, I wasn't wearing enough to take off. I did a dance."

"I'll bet you were pretty good, too."

"I wasn't bad. I did a sort of harem dance." She stood up and executed a few steps, swinging her hips stiffly. "My name was Vera Valentine—my professional name, that is. My real name was Vera Foster."

"I'll have to brush up on my dancing, I can see that," George said.

Mrs. Bigelow began to pack up her equipment. "If you'll help me back to the house with this stuff, I'll show you the picture I did yesterday."

Chapter Three

O H, we're going to have such a lovely summer!"
Dolly said, pausing to gaze out at the flowering
pear tree in the garden. She was standing beside
Homer's desk arranging some apple blossoms in a blue
bowl. The angular beauty of the branches with their pink
buds pleased her, reminded her of a Chinese painting.
She arranged them according to directions she had read in
a magazine, high on one side, low on the other.

Eloise, the new daily maid, was cleaning the upstairs
rooms. Since Eloise came, Dolly had found less and less
to do around the house. It was surprising how quickly
she was adjusting to being a member of the leisured class.
Grace, who had moved out with Raymond to the
gardener's cottage for the summer, was not adjusting so
quickly. She already missed the city and her job, which
had kept her in contact with other people.

Homer had taken a few minutes off from gardening to
read his mail. Nowadays, he spent every daylight minute
in the garden with Mr. Newby, digging, pruning, trans-
planting, weeding. He was drunk with gardening. Sometimes he got up in the middle of the night to read his
garden guide, to check whether Mr. Newby was right
about when the roses should be pruned, how to stake
delphiniums, what kind of fertilizer to use on peonies.

A dozen times a day he called Dolly into the garden to share his delight in some marvel of nature: a nesting robin, the masses of blue and yellow irises bordering the terrace, the trilliums flowering untended in shady corners.

Homer had made a number of new friends. The best of these was Frank Gates, chief of the village police, with whom he spent two evenings a week playing checkers. Frank had a good deal of time on his hands, for the villagers were quiet, law-abiding people. If any disturbance did occur, he sent out what he called "one of the boys," meaning his lone assistant.

Homer's literary career had been postponed for the time being. On the desk in front of him, pushed well into a corner, was his tablet of ruled paper. *The Body in the Well* had never got beyond the opening sentence, but he had every intention of going on with it, once the heavy spring work in the garden was finished. He had even consulted Frank Gates on certain technical aspects of police investigation, and had asked him what he thought of the title and the plot. "Sounds great," Frank had said. "Give me a good murder any day in the week."

"When I think of last year," Dolly went on, standing back to see if her arrangement was taking proper shape, "when we lived in that dark little flat. . . . Did you know, Homer, that I never really saw the spring before? Oh, I knew when it was spring, by the forsythia around the front doors of houses, and that old magnolia tree in the park, but it wasn't the same as here, where you feel it inside, too. I'm not very good at explaining *feelings*," she went on, knitting her forehead in her effort to do so, "but I can't help thinking sometimes that we're not the same people as we were last year—that it was someone altogether different who lived in that flat and worried about bills and what would happen when we grew old."

"Did you worry about that, too?" Homer looked up. "I thought it was only me."

"I don't feel like the same person. In the middle of the night I wake up and I want to run downstairs and turn on all the lights to make sure it's all still here—the new piano and everything."

"I know exactly what you mean," Homer said. "We *are* different people, Dolly. Your mother, too, with her painting and her new beau." He glanced at the framed pictures on the wall. "I'm not so sure about Grace and Raymond," he added after a minute.

"I think Mother's happy, though you never can tell about her. I know *he* is, having someone his own age. . . ." She smiled at the memory of George's cheerful face. "And Grace. . . ." She looked troubled, then said. "I'm sure Grace will be happy here."

"She's asked me to drive her to the station to catch the ten-fifteen."

"A day in town will do her good," Dolly said, and turned again to the sunlit garden, where robins were splashing in the concrete bird bath Homer had placed in the shade of a white birch. "You'd better ask Raymond to come for lunch."

Back in the flat, the thing that had caused her greatest unhappiness was something she had tried to put out of her mind: the knowledge that Homer was a failure. Pretending he was not, making excuses, trying by sheer will power to build him up in the eyes of others, and in her own eyes, too, had become second nature to her. But sometimes when they sat together in the evenings she would look at him and feel a great wave of resentment. He could do better if he tried, she would think. He could study, try to improve himself. But he does nothing.

Evening after evening he just *sits*. And then her resentment would vanish as she realized that Homer knew better than anyone else how far short of his goal he had fallen. She would feel like crying—for him, for herself, for all the poor people of the world. She would wonder if perhaps it was her fault. The magazines were always saying that a man's success or failure depended a good deal on his wife. Dolly would lie awake at night thinking about this, feeling inadequate, dreading the future.

Now all that was in the past. They *were* different people. She was different, and Homer, with his new air of self-confidence, was not that little man who lived in a cheap flat and worried about his job, who used to turn on the television every night the minute he got home, trying to lose himself in a make-believe world. He was someone altogether different.

"I know *I'm* happy," Dolly said. She spoke to an empty room. Outside on the terrace Homer was spading leaf mold into soil for his window boxes.

"What shall we do today?" Grace had asked her husband, earlier that morning.

"Do? I thought we came out here to rest."

"We can't spend the entire summer resting."

"I don't see why not." Raymond pushed back his chair, leaving the breakfast dishes for her to wash up, and went into the living room to lie down.

When Homer had suggested that Grace and Raymond spend the summer in the gardener's house at Dove Cottage she had jumped at the chance. An attack of flu earlier in the spring had left her listless, without ambition. She thought she was tired of people, of the city's bustle, that it would be sheer heaven to do nothing for an entire summer. The little gardener's cottage was as compact as a doll's house. She sublet the flat in town, moved her furniture out to the cottage, and for three days, while she arranged her belongings, had looked forward with pleasure to the summer. Now that she was feeling better, had rested enough, she was beginning to wonder how she would fill her time. She was learning that being tired at night has its compensations, for if you are tired enough you sleep without dreaming.

She spent an hour tidying up the small house, then, to kill time, did her nails and combed her hair a different way. Glancing down at herself, she was suddenly dissatisfied with her suburban clothes, the sweater and skirt and flat brogues which the fashion magazines had assured her were correct for country living. She wanted to feel sleek and modish in high-heeled pumps and her best suit. Before she changed into these, she telephoned her closest friend, Muriel Miller. They arranged to meet in town for lunch, and to spend the afternoon shopping.

"You look peaky," Muriel remarked, with the frankness of a dear friend, as she shook out her napkin. "Shall we have the chicken pie?"

"The salad is less fattening."

"One salad, one chicken pie," Muriel told the waitress. She examined the cutlery, rearranged the centerpiece, and placed cigarettes and matches on the table in readiness. "Or bored," she added. "Perhaps country living doesn't agree with you."

"I haven't been sleeping well," Grace said.

"I could *never* sleep in the country." Muriel spoke as if she were commending some virtue in herself. "All those frogs singing."

"I don't mind it, especially when we're living rent-free."

"Lucky you, with your rich relatives. Will you stay on there permanently?"

"I must go back to my job in the autumn."

"I don't see why, when your sister is perfectly willing to support you. You don't realize how lucky you are. I have nothing to look forward to but Dave's retirement pension, and God knows how we shall live on that. Why can't you sleep?"

"Do you remember Eddie Waite?" Grace asked.

"That old boy friend of yours?"

"I had the silliest dream about him last night." Grace laughed, but a wistful expression crossed her face.

Muriel noticed it. "Do you often dream about old lovers?" she asked.

"Eddie and I were never . . . We were too young, afraid of the consequences. Sometimes, though, we used to go to the park, and lie in the long grass behind the statue of the pioneers."

"I know the place. That was where Dave and I first —where we became engaged, I mean." Though they had no secrets from one another, and spared no details when discussing their husbands, Muriel sometimes tidied up the truth. "Tell me about your dream," she invited, hitching her chair forward and propping her elbows on the table.

"There's nothing much to tell. We were in this room, and I wanted him to make love to me, but he kept turning his back: I can't think why it upset me—such a silly dream."

"Not unusual in women our age." Muriel half-closed her eyes, knowingly. "What other men do you dream about? You can tell me, you know. I understand these things."

"Last week in our neighbor's garden I saw a young

laborer—oh, very handsome, with broad brown should-
ders . . . he was stripped to the waist . . . and lovely white
teeth. Later he came to my door to borrow some tool or
other. He thought, because we live in the gardener's
cottage, that I was the wife of Homer's gardener. He was
foreign, extremely polite. . . . Not an ordinary laborer,
I'm sure."

"And did you dream about him?"

"Yes, that night. And the next morning I carried a
cup of coffee to him—he was just beyond the fence—and
tried to engage him in conversation. I only frightened
him."

"It's obvious what your trouble is: you're a neglected
wife. Wouldn't you think, with all the resting Raymond
does in the daytime. . . ." Muriel stared moodily at her
plate. "What we both need is a change," she said after a
minute. "We ought to have some fun before we're too
old to enjoy it. In France, it's quite usual for women our
age to take lovers."

"But we couldn't," Grace said quickly. "This isn't
France."

"No, I suppose not."

"Besides, we could never find the right kind of man."

"I know what you mean. The nice ones are all happily
married, or they assume that *we* are. And we wouldn't
want the other kind—though there are plenty of them
around—the roving-eyed philandering type, I mean. It
wouldn't mean enough to them. We could never be sure
they weren't consoling another unhappy wife the next
night."

"I didn't say I was unhappy."

"Of course not. I am not *un*happy, myself. I'm simply
bored."

"You've always said Dave is so attentive."

"Demanding," Muriel corrected. "It's no use falling asleep, or saying I have a headache, so I make the most of it. I pretend it's someone else."

"Who?"

"Oh, various men. Lately it's been the manager of the supermarket on Washington Street."

"Mr. Hanson?"

"Is that his name? The one with the wavy blond hair. I have an idea he looks at me in a rather special way. I make excuses to ask him questions—where are the salted crackers, and so on. I can never find the courage to say anything more significant—to give him a hint of my admiration for him."

"He'd think you'd gone mad. He might call the store detective."

"Yes," Muriel agreed. "Oh, I *hate* being forty!" She pushed her plate aside impatiently, as if she were trying to push back the years as well. "I feel so young inside—younger than I did at twenty. . . . And there's always the danger of making a fool of oneself; of thinking someone cares when they're only being sociable. . . . Will we be like this when we're fifty—still searching for someone to love?"

"We'll be too old to care," Grace said sadly.

Up in the hills beyond the village George Adams and Mrs. Bigelow were having a picnic lunch. They did not sit on the ground, but on folding chairs that George had bought for such occasions, and which he always carried with him, in the back of his new convertible. The purchase of this vehicle had caused his son and daughter-in-law much concern. They thought him an old fool, and wondered if he ought to have his head examined. When, to top everything, they learned—not from him—that he and Mrs. Bigelow had visited a night club in the city, they were deeply shocked. "At their age!" they said to one another. "They're both mad!" Fred even went so far as to invite a friend of his, a psychiatrist, out to the house one night, ostensibly for dinner, but in reality to observe his father's behavior. "He's saner than you are," the friend assured him, but Fred and Lola couldn't believe that. Fred said he hoped to God his father wasn't entertaining any silly ideas about marriage, at his age. "It would be the very thing for him," the friend said. "Give him a new lease on life." "It wouldn't do *us* any good," Fred said, thinking of his father's money.

"What's your favorite color?" George had asked Mrs. Bigelow one day. "In a car, I mean."

"Blue," she decided. "Or a nice bright red. Not black. That one of Homer's looks like a hearse."

A day or so later he had come sailing up the driveway in a low-slung convertible of robin's-egg blue. Mrs. Bigelow gaped with admiration. He had taken her for a drive up over the hills and along the highway, where the wind lifted her hat and carried it miles away across a field.

He came to see her almost every day. On fine mornings they went painting, for George had taken up art in a serious way, too. He had gone to the city one afternoon and bought himself a truly impressive amount of equipment, including a metal case that unfolded to become an easel, twenty large-sized tubes of paint, two dozen brushes, and a folding umbrella of striped canvas. Feeling that he needed instruction, he had persuaded Mrs. Bigelow to accompany him to an art school in the city for a series of lessons, but after the second lesson Mrs. Bigelow decided she was being done more harm than good. The instructor, who was supposed to be a famous artist, insisted upon her doing everything the wrong way. "He's ruining my style," she told George. "All that talk about form and composition—it's nothing but poppy-cock. He'll ruin your style, too."

George felt that he had not yet developed a style—at least, nothing like Mrs. Bigelow's, which everyone agreed was unusual—but he did concede that the lessons were not up to his expectations.

"The only way to learn to paint is to go out and *paint*," Mrs. Bigelow said. "That's the way I learned." She had already completed more than a dozen large canvases, which had been framed and now hung in various rooms of the house. She hadn't mentioned it to anyone yet, but she was turning over in her mind the idea of holding an exhibition in the autumn. By that time, at her present rate, she should have about fifty pictures finished.

Today, they were doing the old falling-down barn with its gaping windows. They sat in the farmhouse garden, long since gone to seed, where nevertheless a few pansies struggled upward through rank grass under the wild roses, and a peach tree was in full bloom. Near by was the old cellar, filled with rubble from the house that had burned down, and overgrown with vines.

They liked doing old buildings—sheds and sway-backed barns—which required no straight lines or vertical edges. George was putting the peach tree in his picture, but Mrs. Bigelow was filling up her edges with green leaves—a nice contrast to the red barn, and giving an impression of looking out through a bower of trees.

When they had finished lunch, they wandered around the old garden, discovering a patch of blue violets under a stone wall. George brushed the dried rabbit-droppings and green willow catkins off the wall and they sat down. A trailing vine caught Mrs. Bigelow's skirt and she ripped it away impatiently. "Everything's so untidy in the country," she complained. "Not like in the park at home where they keep things neat. And I haven't seen one magnolia tree since we moved out here. It hardly seems like spring, without that big old magnolia tree in the park to look at. I used to go out every day it was in bloom."

"We'll drive in tomorrow and look at it," George promised. "What I used to like were the tulips around the city hall, and the pigeons. They used to eat out of my hand."

"And the swans on the duck pond in the park; and those long-legged pink birds."

"Flamingoes."

"That's it. You knew it was summer when they put them out in the pond."

"We ought to go in and paint them."

"It would be a nice change," she agreed.

"Shall we go to the movies tonight?" he asked, taking her hand.

"If you like."

"All the way to the city, or to the one in the village?"

Mrs. Bigelow hesitated. The city had much nicer theaters, and there were places to go afterwards: coffee houses where they could sit and eat toasted buns while they watched the crowds go by; or they might, as they had done on several occasions, drop in somewhere for half an hour's dancing. There was always the chance, too, that some of her city friends would catch sight of her driving by with George in his new car. Hoping this would happen, she usually persuaded him to take a turn along Elm Street, where she had lived. Once she saw two ladies she knew coming out of the drug store. She had waved and waved, but it was not until the car was almost out of sight that it dawned on them who she was, for naturally they had never expected to see her driving by like the Queen of England in an expensive blue convertible, with a handsome man.

She would much prefer driving to the city, but she had neglected Dolly shamefully of late, leaving her as good as alone—with only Homer for company—so many evenings. Of course it was less lonesome for Dolly, now that Grace and Raymond had moved out, but they might consider themselves neglected, too. "The village," she decided. "And let's catch the seven o'clock show, so we'll be home early."

"The village it is, then. I'll call for you right after dinner." George gazed off at the landscape, but his free hand crept over and rested on her leg.

"Fresh!" she said, slapping his arm. But she did not move away, or withdraw her other hand from his.

At ten o'clock that night, Homer, driven indoors at last by fatigue and darkness, was dozing by the fire in the study. It was a warm night, and there was really no need of a fire, but Dolly loved the cheerfulness of the leaping flames, as he did, too, though the heat sent him to sleep. Mrs. Bigelow and George had returned from the movies, and now they were in the living room with Dolly giving a concert. Dolly was playing the piano, Mrs. Bigelow was strumming the mandolin and singing as well, George was singing. He had been discovered to possess a passable voice, somewhere in range between a tenor and a baritone. The song was "Darktown Strutter's Ball," one of Mrs. Bigelow's favorites.

"Now let's have 'Kathleen Mavourneen'," George said.

In the study, Homer half woke, listened for a moment to the ringing tones, then sank back into sleep. George was a real Irish tenor in the high notes.

When George had finished his song, Dolly slipped out to the kitchen to bring in the sandwiches she had prepared earlier. On the way back she glanced in at Homer, saw that he was asleep, and closed the door so that he would not be disturbed.

In sleep, Homer was half dreaming, half sorting through his treasure chest of contentment. He felt some-times that he had just about as much happiness as he could handle, for he had been out of practice so many years. His needs, as he had told Mrs. Bigelow, were not great. He had no more than a mild ambition to appear important in other people's eyes, or to keep up with those ubiquitous Joneses against whom everyone measures success. All he had ever really wanted was to be free from fear, the fear of insecurity, of poverty in his old age. It was fear of not doing his job as well as he was expected to do it that had made him dread going to the bank each morning. He was always waiting for the day when he would be called into the manager's office and told his salary was being cut, or that a younger man had been found to replace him. To know that he would never again be dogged by fear was pure bliss.

The sound of knocking awakened him. Thinking it was someone at the front door he turned over, waiting for Dolly to answer it, but the murmur of voices in the living room went on without interruption. Then the knock came again. It was someone at the door leading to the terrace. Homer sat up.

Then the door opened and a thin-faced man, wear-ing a dirty cream-colored linen suit, stepped into the room.

Homer rose bravely to meet him. "What do you want?" he asked.

"Now, don't get excited. It's only me. I was going to the front door, then I saw you had company, so I came around here."

"Who are you?"

"Oh, come on, now, Homer, you know who I am." The unshaven face widened in a smile.

"I never saw you before."

"Take another look." The man turned his face from side to side, giving Homer a view of both profiles. Shaved and washed, he might have been handsome, but not in a way that Homer admired. He wore, instead of a tie, a red silk muffler knotted around his throat and tucked into his open shirt front. This, combined with his high cheekbones and a half-smiling look about his mouth—as if he had a joke up his sleeve—gave him what Homer could only describe as a Bohemian appearance. An artist down on his luck, but still full of confidence. Homer could see that the suit had once been expensive, though now it was soiled and even torn under one arm.

"See anything familiar?" he asked, facing Homer again. "How about this scar, then?" He pushed back some strings of brown hair to show a diamond-shaped scar on one temple. His fingers were long and tapering, though the nails were edged with black. "That give you a clue?"

Homer shook his head.

"Sure?" The man stuck his hands in his pockets, smiling, prolonging the game.

"I don't know you," Homer stated with finality. He had often thought how he would deal with a burglar if the need arose; he had never considered the possibility of having to deal with an escaped lunatic, which he was beginning to suspect this man was.

"Well, I'm certainly disappointed. I thought for sure you'd know me, Homer." The man waited another minute, then, as if unable to bear the suspense himself, he brought the game to an end. "I'm *Claude*!" he cried. "I'm your cousin Claude."

"Oh, no!" Homer took a step backwards. "Claude went over Niagara Falls in a barrel."

"That's what everyone thought. That's what I wanted them to think. But you should know I'd have more sense than to do a thing like that, Homer." Claude sat in a chair beside the fire and flung one knee over the other, making himself at home. "Oh, I'm Claude, all right," he said in an affable, reassuring voice. "Matter of fact," he added, rubbing one hand over his face, "the way I look, I never expected you to recognize me—not after thirty years."

"I don't believe you are Claude," Homer said flatly. "Claude was taller. Anyway, he's dead."

Claude's face darkened for a moment. "Listen, if I say I'm Claude Jeffries, I *am*. You understand?"

"Can you prove it?"

"I could, if I wanted to take the trouble."

"What are you doing here?"

"What am I doing here? Well, I like that. You're my only living relative, aren't you?"

"But why come back now? Why not a year ago, when your mother—when Aunt Harriet died? Why wait all this time?"

"I didn't even know she was dead, let alone with all that money. I've been out of touch with things." This remark struck Claude as grimly amusing, and he gave a short laugh. "I only heard about it a week ago, so the first thing I said to myself was, 'I'd better have a talk with old Homer.' So here I am."

"What are you going to do now?"

"I'm going to visit with you folks for a while, till we can work something out. First thing I'm going to do, as soon as those people leave, is get your wife to cook me a big dinner. Then I'll take a bath and go to bed."

"We can't put you up. We haven't room."

"You'll find room," Claude said calmly. He leaned back, linked his hands behind his head and surveyed the room with a proprietary air. "You recognize the scar, now that you know who I am?" He pulled the hair back from his temple again.

Homer did recognize it. He felt dizzy, and for a moment was afraid he might faint. The voice of George saying good-night at the front door was suddenly the voice of Mr. Harris at the bank, saying, "Sorry, Homer, no openings. We're taking on younger men only."

"Any cigarettes?" Claude asked.

"I don't smoke."

"You'd better order some, first thing in the morning." Claude took from his pocket a sack of tobacco and some papers. He rolled the cigarette with one hand. "Remember the time I got kicked out of school for setting fire to the toilets?" he asked in the amused reminiscent voice of one recalling childish pranks.

Dolly opened the door. "Oh, you're awake, Homer. Do you want some tea?" She stopped so short that Mrs. Bigelow, coming up behind, almost fell over her. "Who's that, Homer?" she asked in a startled voice.

"Come in, Dolly. You might as well know. He says he's my cousin Claude."

"There's no 'he says' about it. I am," Claude said pleasantly. He lounged to his feet, waiting to be introduced.

"Your cousin?"

"Aunt Harriet's son."

"But he's dead!"

"I *thought* he was dead. I thought he went over Niagara Falls in a barrel."

"This your wife, Homer?" Claude bowed with elaborate politeness in Dolly's direction. "And who is *this*?" he asked, turning his smile on Mrs. Bigelow.

"My mother," Dolly answered mechanically.

"What is she doing here?"

Mrs. Bigelow was pulling herself together after her first surprise. "I live here, that's what I'm doing. More to the point, what are *you* doing?"

"I certainly like everybody's attitude," Claude complained, but in a chaffing way, as if he saw the joke, if they did not. "Here I am Homer's long-lost cousin come back from the dead, and what kind of a reception am I getting?"

Mrs. Bigelow looked him over. "You're no more Homer's cousin than the man in the moon. You're an imposter. You've come here to rob us. Homer never had a cousin. *I* never heard you mention any cousin, Homer."

"I was the black sheep of the family," Claude explained. He laughed.

"We all thought he died years ago," Homer told his mother-in-law.

"*Thought* he died? Don't you know?"

"Aunt Harriet got word that he drowned."

"Then what makes you suppose he didn't?"

Homer said nothing.

"That's it, take his word for it! Allow yourself to be taken in by every Tom, Dick and Harry who comes along claiming to be your cousin. I suppose it's dawned on you what he's after."

"Yes, I know," Homer said.

"He wants your money. He'll be saying next that the money your Aunt Harriet left you belongs to him."

"You're catching on fast," Claude said, clapping his hands and giving her a congratulatory smile.

"And you're so spineless you'd believe him. If I were you I'd call the police."

Homer did not move.

"You—Doll—is that your name?" Claude turned to Dolly. "Can you get me something to eat? Any steaks in the house?"

Dolly swallowed and shook her head. "There's some stew left over from dinner."

"That'll do. I've eaten worse things than stew. Go heat it up, will you?"

"Don't you move, Dolly!" Mrs. Bigelow commanded. "Allowing a perfect stranger to come in here and order your wife around like a common servant!" she scolded Homer. "You ought to be ashamed! If you're afraid to call the police, I will."

"Go ahead." Claude's amiable expression did not change. "Go ahead and call them. Just remember, though, that when they find out who I am, it'll be you they'll kick out, seeing you're all living on money that rightfully belongs to me. Isn't that so, Homer?"

Homer stared dejectedly at the wall and made no answer.

"Now, then, how about that stew?" Claude led the way to the kitchen.

They looked at one another, then followed him. Mrs. Bigelow cast a glance at the telephone in the hall.

"They'd prove you were an imposter and clap you in jail," she said.

"What if they didn't?" Claude pulled a chair up to the kitchen table and watched Dolly as she put the stew on to heat, cut bread, and set out dishes and flatware. He buttered a slice of bread and ate it. Mrs. Bigelow and Homer stood with folded arms, watching Dolly's movements as if she were performing some conjurer's trick.

"That's hot enough," Claude decided after a time, holding out his plate. He ate ravenously. "Say, this is delicious! You're a pretty good cook, Doll. We're going to get along okay, I can see that."

"But why come to us?" Homer asked suddenly. "Why not see a lawyer?"

"That's a sensible question," Claude conceded. He passed his plate for a second helping of stew and ate steadily for some minutes. "I'll tell you why I didn't go to a lawyer, Homer," he said at last. "But, first, I want you to understand that I didn't come here to make trouble. I'm good-natured, see? Easy to get along with. I have no wish to put you out of your home unless I'm forced to." He sopped up the last of the gravy with a piece of bread, but in a mannerly way, using a fork. "That was good," he told Dolly. "Now, a piece of pie would hit the spot, and some coffee."

"There's tea. . . ."

"Tea will do." He shrugged his shoulders in a good-humored way.

When he had eaten the pie and drunk two cups of tea he hitched his chair around and rolled a cigarette. "Now let's get down to business," he said, pushing his empty plate aside and tilting back with one elbow resting on the table. "Let's talk things over. I take it you all agree that if my mother had known I was alive, she'd have left her money to me; or, if she didn't leave it to me—if, as actually happened, she left no will, and if the lawyers hadn't thought I was dead, I'd have got the money anyway, being her nearest relative. Everybody agreed on that?" He looked sharply at each of them. His eyes were light brown, almost yellow, with stubby black lashes.

Dolly gave a little frightened nod of her head, Homer averted his eyes, and Mrs. Bigelow stuck out her lower lip as if she disdained to consider such a possibility.

"Now, you're wondering why I don't go to a lawyer, prove my identity and collect my inheritance, right?"

"It would seem the logical thing to do," Homer said.

"I'll give you the whole story." Claude tapped ashes into his empty cup. "Everybody thought I drowned going over Niagara Falls in a barrel, correct?"

Homer nodded.

"Well, it wasn't me in the barrel, it was a sack of grain. I'd got into a little trouble. . . . *Little* trouble!" Claude chuckled mirthlessly. "That's the understatement of the year."

"With the police?"

"Who else? I didn't fancy spending the rest of my life in a government guest house—or worse." His face darkened. "So I rigged up this scheme about going over the falls in a barrel. The fellow that helped me with it is still around." He paused, making sure they understood the significance of this statement. "We figured there wouldn't be anything left of the barrel by the time they fished it out of the river below the Falls, and everybody would think I'd drowned. So, sure enough, that's what happened. Not such a dumb idea, was it? It was in all the newspapers. Big headlines: 'Daredevil Meets Death,' 'Cataract Claims Another Victim.' Front page stuff."

"Was it you sent those newspaper clippings to Aunt Harriet?"

"Nobody else but," Claude said, pleased with himself.

"But that was fifteen years ago. Where have you been since then?"

"Here and there." Claude waved one hand vaguely. "The point is, I could go to a lawyer—any lawyer— tomorrow, and prove my identity. Fingerprints, and so on. The fellow who helped me rig up the barrel would testify. I'd have no trouble proving who I am. So, before long, I'd get all this money you're living on, Homer. You'd be out selling pencils on street corners."

Dolly put her hands over her eyes.

"There's one catch." Claude ground his cigarette out in a saucer and rolled another. "I'm going to be perfectly honest with you. I'm going to lay my cards on the table. The minute I prove I'm Claude Jeffries, the police will move in. I'd spend the next twenty years behind bars. *However*," he raised his voice as Homer was about to say something, "there's no law saying a man can't inherit money because he happens to be in jail. You know of any such law?"

"I know very little about such things."

"Take it from me, there's no such law. Now, the way I look at it, Homer, we're both in a spot."

"*You're* in a spot," Mrs. Bigelow said, but in a small voice.

"So here's what we'll do. I'll stay on here with you folks, share my inheritance with you. In return, you'll protect me, keep my true identity a secret. If anyone asks, you can say—oh, let's say I'm a boyhood friend of yours, we grew up like brothers, old buddies . . . hold on a minute," he interrupted himself. "That doesn't sound quite right. You're ten years older than I am. Well, we can say you were like an *older* brother to me."

"How long were you thinking of staying?" Homer asked.

"How long?" Claude looked at him as if he had asked what made the sun rise. He made no answer, but went on with his instructions. "You'll call me Mr. Richards. Mr. Claude Richards."

"What name have you been using all these years? You couldn't have called yourself Claude Jeffries when he was supposed to be dead."

"I've had various names," Claude said airily.

"You're not in trouble with the police now, for any recent misdemeanor?"

Claude frowned. "You trying to be nosey or something?"

"I was merely curious."

"Well, don't be. Just remember I'm doing you a big favor. Now, then——" He got back to the business at hand. "Here's what you'll tell your friends. You'll say I'm Claude Richards, an old friend of Homer's. I'm a writer. I write stories about foreign countries—mountain climbing in Tibet, pearl diving in the South Seas—that sort of thing. You haven't seen me for—oh—twenty years, Homer, because I've been travelling in all these foreign countries. I've just got back from South Africa— big game hunting. Everybody got that straight? You got that straight, Auntie?"

Mrs. Bigelow set her mouth in a stubborn line.

"What's my name?" He stared at her until she had to look at him.

"*You* say it's Claude Richards."

"Right." He placed his palms on the table and prepared to rise. "Oh, one thing more. Anybody live here besides you three?"

"Dolly's sister and her husband are staying in the gardener's cottage at the end of the garden."

"What about servants?"

"They come by the day. We have a combination odd-jobs man and gardener, and a daily maid."

Claude considered this. "Just make sure they get the story straight. There's no need to warn you what will happen if you give the game away—to anyone." Once more he stared intently at each of them in turn, until they were forced to meet his eyes. "To *anyone*," he repeated. "Even your sister, Doll."

Dolly's hands trembled as she stacked up the dishes he had used. A saucer fell in the sink and broke.

"Well. . . ." Claude yawned. "I'll clean up and go to bed. I'm tired. No need for you all to come up," he said as they began to trail up the stairs behind him. "I can find my way around." He looked into all the bedrooms. "This one will do."

"That's *my* room!" Mrs. Bigelow cried indignantly.

"Your room, is it?" He gave her a sidelong smile, as if he meant to have some fun at her expense. Then he changed his mind. "Hell, I'm not hard to get along with. Who's in this next room?"

"That's the spare room."

"It'll do." He made for the bed. Dolly ran in and snatched off her lace bedspread a second before he lay down. "This is fine," he said, lying back with his hands behind his head and his legs stretched out. "Now, you get me a couple more pillows, Doll, and a pair of Homer's pyjamas, and I'm all set."

"Haven't you got a suitcase or anything?" Homer asked.

"I travel light." Claude closed his eyes. "You folks can mosey along now. I'll be perfectly comfortable here. Just make sure there's plenty of hot water for a bath, and lots of towels. As soon as I get cleaned up I'll crawl under these sheets and sleep like a baby." He called after them as the door closed, "Nighty-night, all!"

They filed downstairs and shut themselves up in the kitchen.

"Putting his dirty shoes on my clean sheets!" Dolly said, bursting into tears.

"I know what I'd do if *I* was head of this house," Mrs. Bigelow said. "I certainly wouldn't stand around meek as a lamb while a perfect stranger came in and took possession. He was going to sleep in *my* room, if you please, and I didn't hear you make a word of protest, Homer. You'd have let him. Are you afraid of him?"

"Yes, I am."

Dolly, who had been drying her tears, caught her breath.

"I'd certainly be ashamed to admit it. Allowing a perfect stranger to come in here, order your wife around like a common servant, and try to put me out of my bed . . . !"

"He's not a perfect stranger."

"You mean you *believe* that pack of lies about him being your cousin?"

"Yes."

"Just because he says he is? How do you *know*?"

"He showed me a scar on his forehead. Claude used to have a scar, where Aunt Harriet hit him once with a shovel—a little brass shovel that she used to keep beside the fireplace. He was about twelve then. He'd taken one of her pottery figurines and sold it to buy cigarettes. He was always light-fingered. I'm not surprised the police want him."

"A great many people have scars. That's no means of identification."

"There are other things, too. Mannerisms, the way he talks. . . . He hasn't changed much. As soon as he said who he was, I recognized him."

"Supposing he *is* your cousin; if the police want him, why not let them have him? Why not telephone

Frank Gates and have him send one of the boys over?"

"And risk going to the poorhouse?"

"He could take everything away from us!" Dolly wept. "We'd have to go back to that flat. We couldn't even go back *there*. We couldn't pay the rent. All this. . . ." She looked around the kitchen, but she was really seeing the whole house, the new piano in the living room, the rugs and curtains she had spent so many happy hours picking out. "Could he really take all this away from us, Homer?"

"The money rightfully belongs to him, since he is Aunt Harriet's son."

"I won't give it up!" Dolly cried vehemently. "I don't care if it does belong to him. He doesn't deserve it." She pushed her hair back from her tear-stained face. "I couldn't stand being poor again."

To soothe her, and because he needed something to cling to, Homer took her hand. "Then what had we better do?" he asked.

"We'll do as he says. He can stay here. I'd rather put up with him than give up our lovely home—and your garden, Homer. I'd rather die."

"Don't cry, Dolly; we'll think of something." Homer went on patting her hand. "If only there was some way to get rid of him," he said, looking around desperately.

"Like pushing him off a cliff?" Mrs. Bigelow asked.

"I'd do that, even, if I thought I could get away with it. I think I'd do almost anything."

"We might try poison; but what would we do with him afterwards?"

"Stop *talking* that way!" Dolly begged.

"I am only trying to be helpful," her mother said. "If anything happened to him it wouldn't be our fault—

an intruder forcing his way in. I don't suppose there's a gun in the house?"

"There must be an easier way than that." Homer spoke as if she had offered a perfectly reasonable suggestion.

Dolly covered her ears. "You're talking nonsense, both of you. Oh, why did this have to happen, when we were so happy?" Her tears, which had not quite stopped, began to flow again.

"You're giving up too easily," her mother said. "You're giving up without a struggle. If I had my way, we'd at least *try* to do something."

"Such as what?"

"I don't know. I'd think of something." Concentrating on the problem, Mrs. Bigelow failed to notice that Homer was appealing to her, something he had never done before. "I don't suppose you could speak to Frank Gates—as a friend, I mean, not as a police officer . . . ?"

"No, I couldn't do that."

"Then why not go to those lawyers, and ask them what to do?"

"The risk is too great. Do you realize, Mother, what it would mean if Aunt Harriet's inheritance were taken from us? I might be able to get back my old job at the bank, though I doubt it. I've already lost my retirement pension, in any case. We'd have to scrimp and save and pinch pennies for the rest of our lives. We'd go back to living in a cheaper flat than the one we left. Dolly's piano would have to go, you'd have to give up painting. . . ."

"Not my painting!"

"You couldn't afford to keep on with it."

"I couldn't give up my painting." Mrs. Bigelow felt confused and a little shaky at the thought, for that would mean giving up her outings with George, and showing off to her friends when they drove into the city.

76

"There's no need to give it up." Homer tried to speak encouragingly. "All we have to do is treat Claude as a guest."

"But what will we tell people? How will we explain his presence here?"

"We must make people believe that he really is a friend of mine—a family friend as he suggested."

"Will they believe that?"

"We must make them believe it. We mustn't tell anyone the true facts—not even Grace and Raymond."

"We were going to have such a happy summer!" Dolly said. "He will become more and more demanding . . . wanting money. . . . He already treats us as if we were the intruders."

"There's no escaping the fact that the money does belong to him."

"No, there's no escaping it," Mrs. Bigelow said. Her own words sounded so ominous that her courage melted away. An air of impending disaster filled the room.

"I know one thing." She spoke bravely for Dolly's sake. "He'd better not try any more nonsense with me. Trying to put me out of my own bed!"

Chapter Four

IN the morning Claude came down to breakfast wearing the blue silk bathrobe Dolly had given Homer for his birthday in April.

"Lucky you're just my size," he said cheerily, seating himself at the table where Homer and Mrs. Bigelow were already eating. "The slippers are a bit snug, but they'll stretch." He thrust out one foot to show that he had also helped himself to Homer's best slippers. A white silk scarf was knotted, Ascot fashion, around his neck.

"Morning, Auntie!" He was all good humor. "You slept well, I trust?"

Mrs. Bigelow stared at him. Bathed and shaved, with his hair washed and his nails trimmed, he in no way resembled the unkempt man who had thrust himself upon them last night. He looked natty, quite handsome, a ladies' man; still slightly disreputable, perhaps, but in a superior way, like the son of a British peer going to the dogs. His changed appearance made him seem different in other ways, too. His manners and his way of speaking —which last night she had considered uncultivated and bullying—now seemed merely breezy. She knew his type. He'd be getting the village girls into trouble if they didn't watch him.

"Two eggs," he said to Dolly.

When he had eaten these, along with a pile of buttered toast and several cups of coffee, he pushed back his chair and took a folded slip of paper from his pocket. "Now, the first thing I want you to do this morning, Homer, is pick up a few things in the village. Where do you keep your bank account?"

"In the village bank."

"Good. You can draw out—oh—say two hundred dollars. That should do me for a day or so. Here's a list of things I need: some stuff from the drug store, shoes. . . . Is there a tailor shop in the village?"

"If you need a suit, you ought to go in yourself."

"Not me. I'm keeping out of sight for a day or so, until I make sure nobody's on my trail. I'm going to sit in the garden and watch the birds. Never mind the suit for the time being, then. I'll borrow something of yours— the sports jacket and gray flannels for a start. . . . Who's that?" He lifted a corner of the curtain as a car drove into the yard.

"It's Eloise and Mr. Newby. They work here."

"I don't want them to see me yet. I'll go upstairs. You can tell them I'm under the weather. Tell them I've got a touch of jungle fever. Now, then, everybody got the story straight—who I am and everything?"

Dolly, who had not touched her breakfast, said "Yes," quickly for all three.

"What say we run through it again, just to be on the safe side?" He stared at Mrs. Bigelow. "What's my name, Auntie?"

She looked sullen, then frightened. "Mr. Richards."

"Go on. What am I doing here?"

"She knows," Dolly said, moving closer to her mother. "We all know what to say."

Claude appeared reassured. "Let's not have any

mistakes, then," he said. "Here's the list, Homer. I want you to drive to the village right away and pick up these things. Bring them up to my room."

Homer, reluctant to leave his womenfolk unprotected for long, drove as fast as he could to the village and bought the articles Claude had requested. He met Frank Gates in the drug store.

"Got that book of yours finished yet, Homer?" Frank asked. He was a good-natured, lazy man, always ready for a chat. "I'm coming over to look at that well one of these days," he continued. "You never can tell, there might be something down there. Just for fun, I looked up the records to see if anyone had disappeared around here. There was a fellow turned up missing ten or twelve years ago—an old guy around ninety—but we always figured he got drowned in Fletcher's Lake. He liked to fish. You got time for a cup of coffee?"

"I'm in a rush today, Frank. Some other time."

"Got to get back and spray the roses, I guess?" Frank laughed. "Dig up the cutworms, weed the turnips, transplant the daisies. . . . If you don't win the garden prize this year it won't be your fault."

Claude was still in his room when Homer returned. He stayed there all day. At noon Homer carried his lunch up on a tray.

Claude was lying on the bed with his head wrapped in towels. "Can you get me something to read?" he asked. "A good travel book, say? I like stories about foreign countries."

In his mother-in-law's room Homer found a library book dealing with the French Riviera.

"That's the ticket," Claude said. "The French Riviera. Now, there's a place you ought to visit. Meet the international set."

"Have you been there?" Homer inquired.

Claude was put out at being questioned. "I haven't been to the North Pole, either," he said testily.

Eloise was curious about the visitor from Africa. She at once pictured a sun-tanned gentleman in a white tropical suit and a pith helmet, such as she had seen in movies.

"Will he be staying long?" she inquired of Mrs. Bigelow, who remained at home all that day to protect Dolly.

"It depends," Mrs. Bigelow said vaguely.

Eloise fetched her purse from the closet and applied fresh lipstick, but she really hoped that Mr. Richards would stay in his room all that day. Knowing the value of first impressions, she did not wish to be seen by him until tomorrow, when, with her hair washed and set, she would be wearing her pink jersey sweater over her new brassière with the pointed cups.

All men interested Eloise, and sometimes puzzled her. She lived with an aunt in the village, but her real home was a farm some ten miles up-country. Before she left home she had been warned so repeatedly about the dangers of being taken advantage of that she had looked forward to spending half her time fending off the advances of her employer, her employer's friends, and any other man who crossed her path. Since nothing had happened, she was beginning to wonder what was wrong. Perhaps she had no appeal for anyone.

Lately she had been going to the movies with Jack Turner, who drove a delivery truck for Pink's Grocery. He had never tried what her mother always called 'monkey business,' though she had thought once or twice that he was about to begin. In the dark theater, while staring intently at the screen, he had seemed to be making preliminary advances. His hand rested as if by accident against her thigh, or, after helping her to arrange her coat against the back of the seat, he slipped one arm around her shoulder. He did this so negligently that he seemed unaware of what he was doing, but allowed one dangling hand to brush against her bosom. When they left the theater, however, when they walked home through the dark lanes and he was free to go ahead without distractions, he made no attempt to do so. She wondered if he thought some distraction was necessary. It did not occur to her that he might be waiting for encouragement, for she had been told that was the one thing men never needed.

"Is Mr. Richards married?" she now asked.

"No, not married."

"Well, I certainly hope he enjoys his visit," Eloise said. She had noticed that both Dolly and Mrs. Bigelow appeared reluctant to discuss their visitor, and she put this down to the fact that he was someone of importance. Since he was a writer, he might want to put her, Eloise, in a book. She spent much longer than usual tidying up the bedrooms that morning, hoping to catch a glimpse of him, but his door remained closed. In Mrs. Bigelow's room she stood before the long mirror gazing at her reflection. She arched her eyebrows and assumed a look of hauteur. "I *beg* your pardon!" she said icily to an imaginary escort. "Kindly keep your hands to yourself." She turned sideways and gave herself a long appraisal from that angle, with her head tilted back and her mouth half open, like her favorite movie star. She tried various smiles: roguish, mocking, tender. She imagined how she would describe herself if she were a writer. She would call herself Rosalind. Rosalind's raven hair was tied with a scarlet ribbon that matched her lips. Rosalind's brown eyes looked up at him, her lovely mouth curved in a smile. The wind strained against Rosalind's gown, revealing the curve of her firm young breasts.

She did not become completely aware of the changed atmosphere in the house until after lunch, when it dawned on her that Homer and Dolly and Mrs. Bigelow had rarely left one another's sides all day. Homer did not work in the garden, Mrs. Bigelow did not go out painting, Dolly did not help with the dusting. If one was in a room, the other two were not far off. They conferred in low tones, exchanged glances, seemed fearful of being overheard, and when she, Eloise, came into the room, they talked about the weather. She did not connect this behavior with the visitor upstairs. She thought everyone was glad to have visitors.

Grace, when she came over from the gardener's cottage, seemed surprised when they told her about Mr. Richards.

"But who *is* he?" she asked, cornering Dolly in the kitchen.

"I told you—a friend of Homer's."

"I never heard of him before."

"Homer hasn't seen him for years. He knew him when he was a boy."

"What is he like? Is he supercilious and highbrow? Most writers are."

"I wouldn't call him highbrow. Quite the reverse."

"Bohemian, then?"

"I really don't know him well enough to say. You will have to judge for yourself."

"You all seem so reluctant to talk about him, I'm beginning to wonder. . . . Don't you like him?"

"I have only known him since last night."

"I'm dying of curiosity," Grace said. "Eloise, have you met this handsome stranger?"

Eloise shook her head. "He's been in his room all

day." She added after a moment, "Nobody told me he was handsome."

"Oh, but he must be. Handsome, mysterious, fascinating. . . ."

"He is none of those things," Mrs. Bigelow said, coming in from the hall where she had been keeping an eye on the stairs. "He's what you'd expect a friend of Homer's to be—dull and commonplace."

"How disappointing," Grace said, and Eloise felt that she spoke for her, too.

"Why is it disappointing, might I ask?"

"I was hoping to have someone to talk to."

"You have Raymond."

"Someone interesting, I mean."

Mrs. Bigelow understood what Grace meant. She and her husband had run out of conversation on their honeymoon. But she frowned and said, "A fine way, to speak of your husband!"

"Surely Mr. Richards can't be so dull, if he's a writer, if he's done all that travelling," Grace insisted.

"You'll find him dull as ditchwater," Mrs. Bigelow assured her. "A common little man; not at all the sort of person you would admire. You'll appreciate your husband more when you've had a look at *him*."

Grace eyed her mother suspiciously. "Why are you trying so hard to convince me he's not worth knowing?"

"I'm simply telling you what he's like." Mrs. Bigelow assumed an expression of exaggerated innocence.

"I'll reserve judgment until I've seen him. What you've been saying only convinces me that he *is* fascinating, and certainly mysterious." From the doorway Grace added, "I may drop in later, wearing my new silk print."

"I wouldn't bother dressing up to impress him," Mrs. Bigelow warned.

But Grace laughed and waved and ran along the path. Dolly and Mrs. Bigelow exchanged looks, then went into the study to confer with Homer.

Eloise strained her ears, but could not hear what they were saying. She had got the impression, too, that Mrs. Bigelow was for some reason trying to make Mr. Richards appear less attractive than he really was, and she was more curious about him than ever. Perhaps he enjoyed a reputation as a lady-killer, like those dashing bachelors in movies who thought nothing of making love to their best friends' wives; or he might resemble the handsome stranger often seen in Westerns, who came riding out of nowhere to a lonely ranch, stayed long enough for the rancher's wife to fall in love with him—and he with her —and then, having changed the lives of all he came in contact with, rode off into the sunset, never to be seen again. Either type, Eloise supposed, was one that a mother would want to protect her daughter from; mothers being the way they were.

She daydreamed all afternoon, inventing situations in which she appeared to advantage.

Mrs. Bigelow's thoughts during the afternoon had run along different lines. The situations she invented were ones in which, by cleverness and quick thinking, she had got the upper hand over their unwelcome guest and sent him packing.

She imagined herself pointing toward the door with fine dignity, saying, "If you are not out of this house within half an hour, Mr. Whatever-your-name-is, I shall call the police." And this time, seeing that she really meant business, he went off with his tail between his legs. As the day progressed she became more inventive, recalling various accidents she had read about in the newspapers. People often tripped over loose rugs and pitched headlong down flights of stairs. They fell out of windows. They took poison by mistake. They ate toadstools instead of mushrooms. They accidentally shot themselves while cleaning supposedly unloaded pistols. She had read of one case where a woman died after eating a sandwich filled with rat poison, which she had mistaken for peanut butter. Of another where a man fell down an unused well and was not discovered for six months.

"Did you ever get around to filling up that old well in the cellar?" she asked Homer.

"No. Why?"

"I just wondered."

They heard Claude stirring upstairs. He ran water in the bathroom, made several trips between his own room and Homer's.

"Is he coming down for dinner?"

"He didn't say."

"I wonder if he is fond of mushrooms?" Mrs. Bigelow mused.

"I know nothing about his likes and dislikes," Homer said impatiently.

"I merely asked a civil question. There's no need to bite my head off."

"We're all on edge today." Dolly tried to smooth things over.

Homer apologized immediately. Mrs. Bigelow did not feel the least bit apologetic, for who was to blame for everyone being on edge, if not Homer? Claude was his relative. There were no criminals in *her* family.

"We must try to be calm," Dolly said. At the beginning of any catastrophe she went to pieces and had a good cry, then later on she settled down and presented to the others an example of sensible composure. "We must try not to let his being here upset us."

They had been listening all day for sounds from upstairs, with a feeling that time had stopped, hung suspended, waiting for Claude to decide when it should go on. When they saw other people behaving naturally— Mr. Newby mowing the lawn, Raymond lying under a tree beside the gardener's cottage reading, Grace, now wearing a full-skirted silk dress and suede pumps, cutting lilacs for a bouquet—they were surprised, then felt sad as they remembered that only yesterday *they* had been free to enjoy themselves.

Around four o'clock, Lola Adams dropped in to collect money for the village library fund, and Dolly was forced, out of politeness, to ask her in for a cup of tea. The invitation was accepted. Then Grace and Raymond wandered in, also on the lookout for food and drink.

"But we really came to see Mr. Richards," Grace confessed.

"He is lying down in his room," Dolly said, and hoped he would stay there. "He has been ill, and has been advised to take plenty of rest in bed."

"We have a celebrity in our midst, you know," Grace told Lola. "Mr. Claude Richards, the famous author and explorer."

"You mean he's staying here?" Lola turned to Dolly with a new look of respect.

"He arrived last night," Dolly said, and then, feeling that something more was needed, she added, "He is a friend of Homer's."

Lola's admiring gaze now turned on Homer. "Imagine being so modest about it—not telling anyone you were a friend of his, a famous person like that!"

"I didn't realize he was that famous." Mrs. Bigelow

fixed Lola with a look of mistrust. "I must say I never heard of him until he arrived unexpectedly last night; but then I'm not much of a reader."

"I try to keep up with the latest books," Lola admitted with a touch of pride. "I recognized his name the minute you mentioned it."

Mrs. Bigelow's eyes sharpened. She disliked Lola intensely, and would like nothing better than to lead her into making a fool of herself. "You've read his books, of course," she remarked, holding out her cup for Dolly to fill. Her voice, her expression, managed to suggest that Lola had better say yes, or brand herself the veriest low-brow.

Homer shifted uncomfortably and tried to divert the conversation by dropping a biscuit.

Lola would not be diverted. "Oh, yes," she answered promptly. "At least, I'm sure I have. . . . I always read the book reviews in *The Times*."

"What sort of things does he write?" Grace asked.

"Travel books." Mrs. Bigelow spoke without hesitation. "Stories about his adventures in far-off lands—treasure hunting in the South Seas, big game hunting in Africa. He's been all over the world, you know. He's just returned from a safari in darkest Africa."

Lola nodded. "I've read his book about the South Seas. What was it called—*Pacific Paradise*? Something like that. What was it, Homer?"

Homer shook his head and began to stammer something, was saved by the sound of footsteps descending the stairs.

"Is that him?" Grace whispered in the sudden silence.

Dolly's hand, holding the teapot, was suspended in mid-air as if frozen. Some hot tea dribbled into the sugar bowl and she set the pot down hastily.

Claude breezed into the room with the assurance of one who knows his arrival is the highlight of any occasion. He was wearing Homer's good Harris tweed sports jacket and the gray flannels. His hair, which that morning had been neither dark nor light—what could only be described as medium brown—was now bleached to a pale straw color. "Just in time, I see," he said, shaking hands all round as Homer introduced him. He had even bleached his eyebrows, Mrs. Bigelow noticed. They contrasted oddly with his stubby black lashes.

"A pleasant custom, afternoon tea." He smiled expansively and sat down in the chair that Homer had momentarily—he thought—vacated. "It's one of the things I like about England. Everybody there drinks tea at four o'clock."

"I'll get another cup," Dolly said.

"Is there anything else you want?" Eloise asked Dolly in the kitchen. "Anything you'd like me to take in?"

"No, I think not," Dolly said, and failed to notice that this was not the answer Eloise had hoped for.

"I'll be in later for the tray, then." Eloise left the kitchen door half open so that she would miss none of the conversation in the living room. She was supposed to be washing vegetables for dinner, but the water running into the sink made it difficult for her to hear anything else. They can have a late dinner, she thought. It won't hurt them for once. She did not take her evening meal at Dove Cottage, but left with Mr. Newby at five-thirty. ("Office hours," her aunt said, recalling that when *she* had been in service, she had worked from dawn to midnight, with no afternoons off and very little pay. Her words and look implied that all this coddling would not benefit the younger generation.)

Eloise felt that the younger generation could do with a great deal more coddling, including being allowed a glimpse of important guests. A cat can look at a king, she told herself as she took up her position just inside the kitchen door.

"In France, of course, they never drink tea," Mr. Richards was saying. "They drink wine."

"Have you been to the casino at Monte Carlo?" Raymond asked.

"Monte Carlo is not, strictly speaking, in France, you know," Mr. Richards said. "Still, a very nice little town. . . ."

"We've been discussing your books, Mr. Richards." Lola Adams' voice cut across a question that someone else was asking. "We were trying to remember the name of the one about the South Seas. Was it *Pacific Paradise*?"

"You've read *Pacific Paradise*?" Mr. Richards seemed pleased.

"I simply couldn't put it down, once I'd begun it. I found it fascinating."

"What was it about?" Mrs. Bigelow asked the question suddenly, as if she hoped to catch Lola off guard.

Mr. Richards answered. "It was about the South Seas," he said with a smile in his voice.

"Such wonderful descriptive passages. I felt that I was there with you—that I saw those tropical islands, and the natives. . . . You have marvellous descriptive powers, Mr. Richards. You must promise to come and speak to our reading club."

"More tea, Lola?" Dolly interrupted rudely.

"We meet every second Thursday. You will come, won't you?"

"I'd love to, of course, but . . ."

"Next Thursday?"

"You've asked Miss Talbot at the library to speak at the next meeting," Dolly reminded.

"But we can get her any time."

"Mr. Richards can't speak at your club," Mrs. Bigelow said sharply. "He is here for a rest. He is under strict orders not to exert himself in any way. He's got jungle fever."

"You're just saying that!" Lola cried in her high affected voice. Eloise did not have to be in the room to know that she was pouting her lips and rolling her eyes, employing all the little-girl tricks that she mistakenly believed made her irresistible.

"How would you like to have the whole village down with jungle fever? *You're* probably catching it right now."

"You want to keep him all to yourself!" Lola accused. "Have you got jungle fever, Mr. Richards?"

"Don't be alarmed; it's not contagious," Mr. Richards told her. "But I am, as Auntie said, under strict orders not to exert myself. The doctor has forbidden me to accept engagements of any sort. I would love to speak at your club, but I'm afraid it's out of the question."

"Perhaps later on?"

"I can't promise."

"The girls will be green with envy when I tell them I've met you," Lola said, and in imagination Eloise saw her crooking her little finger daintily as she sipped her tea.

As soon as the chink of cups had subsided, Eloise smoothed her hair, added a fresh layer of lipstick, and went in to fetch the tray. She was just in time, for Dolly was on the point of rising to bring it out. "Thank you, Eloise," she said in a dismissing voice. Then, as Eloise lingered to wipe a spot of cream off the table and brush away invisible crumbs, she had to say, "Oh, Eloise, this is Mr. Richards."

Eloise said she was pleased to meet him. He smiled
and said, "Hello, Eloise," in the nicest way. His glance
ran up and down her figure, and she was sorry she was not
wearing her pink jersey. However, he seemed to like
what he saw. She felt his eyes following her as she left
the room.

In the kitchen, as she washed the vegetables (for,
having met him, she could now concentrate on this
despised job) she sorted out her impressions. He was
certainly not young, she thought, but he did possess a
good deal of dash, an engaging air of rascality that she
found attractive. She liked fair-haired men, too, and his
hair was pale as corn silk—bleached by the African sun,
she supposed. He looked as though he might be the sort
of man her mother had warned her about so repeatedly.
She hoped he was. It would give her a chance to defend
herself against being taken advantage of, a situation which
she had gathered from her mother's talks must be most
entertaining, though dangerous.

"Oh, he's adorable!" Lola whispered to Dolly as she said
good-by on the terrace. Claude and Homer were still
inside. "I'm going to bring Fred over to meet him." She
squeezed Dolly's hand warmly, then hurried home to
telephone her friends.

"Adorable!" Mrs. Bigelow mimicked, staring after her.
"She hasn't got much up here, that woman." She tapped
her forehead as she turned to the others and said with a
sharp glance at Grace. "I hope you don't think he's
adorable."

"Yes, I do. I think he's cute."

Raymond scowled. "I don't see anything *cute* about him."

"Rather handsome, I thought," Grace said perversely.
"I liked his hair. You don't often see men with such pale

blond hair. I suppose it's from being in the sun so much."

"You've got no more taste than that one has." Mrs. Bigelow threw a glance of disgust at the hedge where Lola had disappeared.

"He's got a good opinion of himself," Raymond said. "I didn't like the way he looked at you," he added, speaking to Grace.

"How did he look at me?"

"Don't pretend you didn't notice. You were lapping it up."

"I don't know what you're talking about," Grace said in a tone of cold annoyance.

"Oh, no!"

"You must admit that he's had some interesting experiences. Have *you* ever shot tigers in Africa?"

Mrs. Bigelow sniffed. "He's probably never set foot in Africa. He was probably repeating something he read in a book."

"Why do you say that?" Grace asked.

But Mrs. Bigelow had received a warning look from Dolly. "Now, you must run along home and cook Raymond's supper," she admonished gaily trying to throw them off the scent. "Fatten him up. Give him lots of eggs and cream." She shooed them down the steps.

As soon as they were out of sight she turned to Dolly and said, "*Now* what are we going to do? That fool Lola will spread the news over the entire village. She's on the telephone right now, informing her friends. 'Mr. Claude Richards, the famous writer.' We'll have to get rid of him before the whole countryside comes traipsing up here to gape at him."

"You didn't help matters, Mother. You led her on. She would never have said she had read his books if you hadn't made her feel that she should have read them."

"I couldn't resist it." Mrs. Bigelow gave a grim chuckle. "*Pacific Paradise*? Of course I've read it," she said in Lola's affected voice. "I'd like to see her face when she learns who he really is."

"She must never know. Mother, you must never tell anyone."

"I have no intention of telling anyone," her mother said sharply. "I'm not a complete ninny, you know." She went into the house, where Claude was asking Homer if there was anything to drink.

There was only some sherry that Dolly had bought for cooking, and used once. Claude pronounced unfit for human consumption, but drank it anyway.

"You must order something tomorrow," he told Homer. "I'll give you a list. You'd all be much healthier if you drank cocktails in the afternoon instead of tea. Better for the system." He sat back, swirling the sherry round and round in his glass. "Quite a nice little party, Doll." He gave her a condescending smile. "I liked your friend Mrs. Adams—the one who had read *Pacific Paradise*. And your sister is a real beauty. I was quite taken with her."

He leaned back more comfortably in Homer's chair. The smile lingered on his face.

Dolly had a headache. She was oppressed by the knowledge that Claude, without any effort on his part, had become definitely established as a welcome visitor, a family friend. The ease with which this had been accomplished frightened her. They had all been so *eager* to accept him. No one had questioned. And she had sat there, dazed and helpless, watching his position being strengthened; had even, by her silence, helped to strengthen it. How will it all end? she asked herself, pressing her fingers to her aching eyes. How *can* it end?

Chapter Five

FOR a week Claude did not leave the house. He slept every morning until noon, and spent the remainder of the day reclining on the terrace, now and then dipping into one of the travel books that Homer fetched from the library. A great number of village women telephoned Dolly, or called on her in person, hoping to be introduced to her famous house guest, but Claude avoided all of them. He instructed Dolly to spread the word that he was not yet well enough to receive visitors.

He had plenty of company, however. Grace and Raymond took to dropping in each afternoon, late, for cocktails. Lola sometimes joined the group, and George, eager to take in anything that looked like a party, was always the first to arrive.

These were gay little parties, too. Eloise ran back and forth with drinks and with trays of exotic canapes which Claude had ordered. Mrs. Bigelow limited herself to one weak cocktail. Homer and Dolly, stubbornly clinging to their tea-drinking habits, were forced to put up with a good deal of affectionate teasing from Claude. This struck Grace and Lola as very sweet and touching.

Claude, lying back in a chrome chaise-longue, entertained the gathering with tales of his adventures. Names of distant places rolled off his tongue; he described far-off lands as if he had spent a lifetime in each one.

"He can't have made up all those stories, surely," Dolly said one morning. "I'm almost beginning to believe them. I find myself thinking that perhaps he has climbed the mountains of Tibet, and spent a winter in Siberia. And written all those books, too. How many did he say—eleven?"

"Fifteen," Homer said. "He's got a list of titles somewhere. *Strange Safari, Arctic Adventure, Treasure Hunting on the Amazon.* . . . I've forgotten what he calls the others. There's one about the Orient, another about a trip around the Horn on a whaler. He certainly makes it all sound convincing."

Mrs. Bigelow sniffed. "He doesn't convince me. How did all this nonsense begin, anyway—this fiction about him being a famous author?"

"You started it yourself, Mother," Homer could not help saying.

She bristled. "I did nothing of the kind."

"You couldn't resist asking Lola if she had read his books, and to make it easier for her, you told her what they were about. You gave her just enough to feed her imagination. Knowing the sort of woman she is . . ." Homer added.

"She's a damned fool, I know that. Oh, yes, it's all my fault. My fault entirely. I take the entire blame."

"Nobody's *blaming* anyone."

"He is not my relative, but I am to blame for his being here, disrupting our lives, turning us all into gin-drinkers, making everyone miserable. I apologize. Perhaps you'd be happier if I went away somewhere. I could get a furnished room in the city. I have my old age pension. I could live on that."

"Oh, Mother!"

"It's all right, Dolly. If Homer doesn't want me here I can go somewhere else. I have no wish to be in anyone's way."

Having got this out of her system, Mrs. Bigelow felt considerably cheered. At dinner that night she asked Claude point-blank how many foreign countries he had visited, and if he had ever actually written a book.

He widened his eyes reproachfully. "You're not suggesting I'd tell a lie, are you, Auntie?"

"Yes, I am."

"Oh, what a thing to say!" He looked at her with an extravagantly wounded expression.

"You haven't answered my question."

His eyes crinkled. "Why don't you ask Lola Adams? She's read my books. Liked them, too."

"Lola Adams hasn't got the sense she was born with."

"Still, I find it very flattering to discover that my books are so well known, even in this out-of-the-way village."

"Why keep up the pretense with us? We all know you never wrote a book in your life, or set foot in any of those foreign countries."

"Mustn't say naughty things!" He shook his finger at her. "Did I ever tell you about the time I travelled down the Nile in a canoe?" he asked in a conversational voice.

"I presume you wrote a book about that, too."

"Oh, yes. I called it"—he paused to think—"*Canoeing Down the Nile*. Not one of my best titles," he admitted after a moment.

"I must read it one of these days," Mrs. Bigelow spoke with sarcasm.

"Yes, you must," he agreed with a bland smile.

Lola Adams telephoned one afternoon, seeking data for a write-up about Claude that she was preparing for the city newspapers.

"But he has asked us to keep his name out of the papers," Dolly protested in a panic.

"Why?" Lola wanted to know.

"Because he is here for a rest. He doesn't want to see people. He doesn't want anyone to know he is here."

"He can rest and see people at the same time."

"His doctor has ordered complete rest and quiet," Dolly said firmly, and felt aghast at her own inventiveness. Until last week she had never told a lie in her life. Now everything she said was a lie. One led to another. "I must ask you not to send anything to the papers, Lola," she said.

"Oh, well, if you insist. . . ." Lola's voice clearly indicated that she thought Dolly was being unreasonable. "But he's coming to my party?"

"I wouldn't count on it, Lola."

"I *am* counting on it. You must make him come, Dolly. When I asked him yesterday he said he would certainly attend, unless he suffered a relapse or something. You must take good care of him."

"You do promise not to send anything to the papers?"

"Of course."

But Lola could not resist sending a small item to the village *Bugle*. This article, under the title "World-Famous Author and Explorer," stated that the famous Mr. Claude Richards would be the guest of honor at a party to be given by Mr. and Mrs. Fred Adams on such-and-such a night.

When the night came, however, Claude was stricken with a recurrence of his jungle fever and was unable to attend. Dolly and Homer stayed at home to look after him, and Mrs. Bigelow stayed to look after them. The reason for Claude's absence from the party was noted in the next issue of the *Bugle*, but its appearance did not calm the ruffled tempers of Lola's acquaintances, who held her responsible for a wasted evening, not to mention money squandered on new gowns.

"Oh, I could just die!" Lola told Dolly the next day. "The way everyone spoke, you'd have thought I knew all along that he wasn't coming."

"He did tell you that the doctor had forbidden it."

"I kept thinking up to the last minute that he *would* come—that he wouldn't disappoint us. I had invited so many people; everyone we knew, including the men from Fred's office and their wives. The house was simply jammed. The liquor cost a fortune. Everybody drank and drank, and the women got cattier and cattier until I wanted to die!"

George and Mrs. Bigelow had a good laugh over the failure of Lola's party. They were laughing for different reasons, but George did not know that. He saw only that Lola had tried to impress her friends and failed. Mrs. Bigelow laughed to cover her anxiety, for Claude was consolidating his position with alarming ease, and the possibility of getting rid of him grew more and more remote. He was taking over, gradually and cunningly, in so many ways making it felt that he was the owner of the house, they the intruders. He did not attempt to do this all at once, was satisfied to accomplish a small triumph each day. The cellar was stocked with fine liquors: whiskies, brandies, wines, gin. He now decided what they should have for meals. The grocery bills mounted. "What's money for?" he asked airily when Homer protested.

Every day or so he said casually, "I'll need a little cash, Homer." A little cash, to him, meant several hundred dollars. He did not spend this—he never went anywhere *to* spend it—but added it to the roll of bills he carried in his pocket.

There came a day, of course, when Homer rebelled. When Claude said, "Going to the village, Homer? You might get me a couple of hundred from the bank," Homer asked him what had happened to the two hundred he had given him yesterday.

"The day before yesterday," Claude said, lying back in his garden chair, blowing smoke rings.

"You can't have spent it. You haven't been anywhere."

"I like to carry a few bills around with me. You know, it's a funny thing, Homer, but I don't feel right unless I've got a pocketful of money. I guess you'd call it a phobia."

His confiding manner as he said this angered Homer. "This has gone far enough," he said. "I'm willing to share my home with you, but I'll be damned if I'm going to keep on shelling out money at the rate I have been. I can't afford it."

"*You* can't afford it?" Claude burst out laughing. "Whose money is it, anyway?"

"It's mine, that's whose it is."

Claude sobered, looked despondent. "Well, Homer, I'm sorry you won't cooperate. I had hoped that we'd get along, but . . ." He shrugged resignedly. "Maybe I'd better go see a lawyer, after all. You know, the more I think of it, the more I think maybe that's the best thing to do. I have a feeling everything will turn out all right for me. I was kind of hoping I wouldn't have to claim my inheritance; for your sake, Homer. I was hoping we could share it. But . . ." He shook his head. "Would they take you on at the bank again?" he asked after a pause, looking up at Homer with candid concern, as if he were willing and anxious to help.

Homer said nothing.

"Well, it's too bad!" Claude sighed. "I sure hate to think of you and Doll and Auntie on your uppers. And that pretty sister-in-law of yours, too, with her sick husband. It's a terrible hardship, keeping the wolf from the door, especially when you're not young any more."

"You seem to forget that the income from the legacy is not large. There's only enough to support us in comfort, not in luxury."

"Perhaps we're foolish trying to share it. Perhaps there's only enough for one." Claude placed his hands on his knees and prepared to rise. "I sure am sorry about this, Homer, but I think the only thing to do is run into town and consult a lawyer. I'll have them send a taxi up from the village."

"How much do you want from the bank?"

Claude looked up, surprised. "Oh, you're going to the bank after all?" He settled back. "Well, then, you might get me a couple of hundred." He picked up a magazine and began to read it. "You're sure you don't mind?" he asked, glancing up.

He allowed Homer to reach the door before he said, "Oh, and Homer, there's something else. . . . Don't you think it's about time we bought a new car? Something with a little more class to it?" As Homer stood with his hand on the doorknob wondering how to deal with this new demand, he added, "No rush about it, of course. Naturally you want time to think it over. We can get prices on the new models and decide tonight."

As soon as the new car was delivered, Claude gave up being a stay-at-home. He spent a day in the city buying clothes—an entire wardrobe. Homer turned pale when presented with the bill for this finery.

"A dozen silk shirts!" he cried. "A *dozen* silk shirts! I never owned one silk shirt in my whole life!"

"I have a very tender skin," Claude said.

"You'll have us in the poorhouse!"

"Always complaining," Claude said gaily. "You're missing half the fun of life with your miserly habits."

After that, each evening as soon as it grew dark, he went for what he called "a little spin" in the new car, returning some time after midnight. No one else used this vehicle. Homer, though it was registered in his name, told Dolly he wouldn't feel right, driving such an expensive model. To pay for it he had been forced to sell some property in the city, for Claude's demands had already used up more than a year's income.

"If this keeps up we'll be poorer than we were a year ago," Homer told Dolly during one of their middle-of-the-night talks. All three, Dolly and Homer and Mrs. Bigelow, spent many hours of each night tossing restlessly, or lying awake staring at the ceiling, searching in vain for ways and means of dealing with Claude's demands.

"He's getting pretty confident," Homer said. "When he first came here he was afraid to poke his nose around the corner. Now he's out every night. If the police are looking for him, he's certainly making himself easy to spot, in that car. Everybody in the village is talking about it." Claude's car—even Homer and Dolly thought of it as his —was sometimes seen in the village, though not often. Usually, he drove toward the city. Where, precisely, they had no way of knowing. The only information Claude vouchsafed about his nocturnal excursions was that they cost a good deal of money.

Attendance at Claude's afternoon cocktail sessions had dropped off. Lola, incensed by his refusal to attend her party—she considered this a deliberate snub—was the first to drop out. Raymond, fed up with tales of adventure, went back to his books, where the adventures took place in English country houses and required less exertion. Then George, not quite knowing what to make of Claude's jocular manner, his expression of sly inner amusement, found a better use for his time. Only Grace was left, having—she said—nothing else to do.

If Claude realized that he was less popular than before, he did not show it. "Always ready with the jokes," as George remarked to Mrs. Bigelow.

"What he calls his sense of humor."

"Well, I've got a pretty good sense of humor myself, but it seems to me he overdoes it. He's the kind who'd see something funny about a funeral. I know he's a friend of Homer's, and all that, still . . ."

"They knew one another years ago."

"People change, I guess," George observed.

"I wouldn't say he's changed for the better," Mrs. Bigelow said. For a moment she was tempted to tell George the whole story. It would be such a comfort to share her anxiety.

"I have an idea Homer doesn't like him too well," George said. "Or Dolly either, for that matter. I can't help wondering why they invited him here. Oh, I guess he's famous, and all that, and I guess famous people think they can act a little different and get away with it."

"He's not that famous."

"That's what Lola's telling people now. She says his books aren't even in the library. You notice that women have stopped pestering Dolly to meet him, or to have him speak at their clubs?"

"Yes, I wondered about that. I thought perhaps they'd got tired of asking." Mrs. Bigelow thought that if Lola were responsible for the waning interest in Claude, she had done a good turn without knowing it.

"I generally get along pretty well with people,"

George went on, "but I don't mind telling you he rubs me the wrong way sometimes. The way he's always kind of teasing, as if he thought everyone but him was kind of half-witted or something. . . ."

Should I tell him? Mrs. Bigelow wondered, and decided that she could not. It would only worsen the situation. George would become anxiously protective, declare that *he* would do something if nobody else had the courage to act. He would bounce in and upset the whole applecart. All through the goodness of his heart, of course. He would mean well.

"Let's talk about something more pleasant," she said.

"That suits me." George pulled her close to him and kissed her cheek. "Listen, why don't we get married?"

In the middle of the night Dolly wakened suddenly. She sat up in bed. A car had driven into the yard and was now backing and turning with a great shifting of gears. Homer stirred. "That's not Claude's car," he said. "What time is it?" He raised himself on one elbow to look at the luminous dial of the bedside clock, which said two-thirty.

"I hear Claude's voice." In the dark, Dolly groped her way to the window. "There's someone with him."

"I hope he hasn't brought one of his gangster friends out here to live," Homer said in a despondent voice.

"It's a truck," Dolly reported. "They're moving something into the cellar."

Homer dragged himself out of bed. He did not want to look. He wanted to stay in bed with the covers over his head, for he had been sleeping without dreaming, for a change, and wanted to go back to this ideal state. By the time he reached the window Claude and a stocky man wearing a leather windbreaker had just disappeared under the porch roof. They could be heard bumping down the cellar steps, apparently carrying some heavy object. At the foot of the stairs they must have run into the water pipes, for a series of dull metallic clunks came up through the radiator.

Dolly had caught a glimpse of the other man. Seen from above, he looked stooped, gorilla-like; as unreal as if he had sprung to life somewhere in the darkened garden, which itself looked threatening now, with its deep shadows and ghostly blossoms under a different pattern of stars. She had never thought of Claude as having friends or accomplices. Now in imagination she saw him backed by a whole army of sinister figures, who would stop at nothing to help him gain his ends. She shivered and dropped the curtain, feeling that she could not stand another night of this slow torturing kind of anxiety. Once you've been happy, unhappiness is much harder to bear, she decided, because then you have something to measure it against.

A sound of hammering came up, and now and then a ring of metal against the water pipes.

Mrs. Bigelow fumbled across the hall, muttering as she bumped into the door.

"Why didn't you turn on the lights?" Homer flicked a switch several times, but nothing happened.

"Perhaps you'd like to turn them on, if you're so smart."

"Are all the lights out?" Homer tried the bedside lamp. "Claude must have blown the fuses."

"Who is that other man?"

"We don't know, Mother," Dolly said.

"It's a wonder your husband doesn't make it his business to find out," Mrs. Bigelow grumbled. "Strangers tramping through the house at all hours, blowing out fuses . . .! For all we know, they might be plotting to blow us up."

"I'm sorry it wakened you, Mother."

"Wakened me? You know very well I never sleep." Mrs. Bigelow revised this statement. "I haven't had a night's sleep since your husband's relative moved in."

"Why don't we all go back to bed?" Dolly suggested. "We can worry about the fuses in the morning."

"With a gang of hoodlums running loose in the house?" her mother asked. As she spoke, the lights came on. She put her hands over her eyes and scurried back to her room, for she never liked anyone, not even Dolly, to see her with her hair in curlers.

In the morning, Homer discovered that the door leading to the furnace room was padlocked.

For a change, Claude came down in time for breakfast. "You won't need that room, now that the furnace is out," he said when questioned, "so I'm using it for my hobby room."

"What is your hobby?"

Claude thought for a moment. "Kind of an experiment, you might say. A creative experiment. I'm making something."

"What?"

"It's a secret. That's why I put the padlock on. No fair peeking, anyone!" he admonished playfully. "I just shoved those tubs of ashes into a corner," he told Homer, "and I moved the fireplace logs out into the laundry room. I knew you wouldn't mind."

"I noticed you blew out some fuses last night."

Claude laughed. "We had a slight accident. It seems we overloaded the fuses when we hooked up a little machine I've got down there—part of my hobby equipment. It won't happen again. We installed some extra doodads to

carry the load. Don't ask me to explain—I'm no elec-
trician. Everyone should have a hobby, Homer," he
added in a patronizing tone. "You should have one
yourself. It would help you to sleep at night."

As soon as he had finished breakfast he said, "Well,
folks, I'm off to my hobby room," and went downstairs.
Some time later the machine started up. At intervals
during the morning it clashed and hummed. Between
times, Claude was apparently making adjustments. He
could be heard hammering, filing, tapping, and occasion-
ally knocking against the water pipes.

Mrs. Bigelow tried to figure out, from the sound of it,
what the machine was being used for. "It's a still for
making liquor," she decided at last.

"He'd need water for that. There's no tap in that
room."

"He could get water from the laundry sink."

"The cellar's full of liquor now. Why should he make
his own?"

"He's going to sell it. He's going to turn this house
into one of those Joe-sent-me places. A speakeasy."

"Speakeasies went out of style thirty years ago."

But Mrs. Bigelow had made up her mind that Claude
was running a still in the cellar. When he came up for
lunch she said to him, "We know perfectly well what
you're doing down there. You're not fooling us for one
minute."

"Nobody can pull the wool over your eyes, Auntie,
we all know that," he assured her.

"I suppose you know it's against the law for a person
to make his own liquor."

He winked at her. "Live dangerously, that's my
motto."

That night after dinner he said, as usual, "Well, folks,

I think I'll take a little spin." Mrs. Bigelow watched him leave, then ran to the cellar to see what she could see. The furnace room was locked tight. She tried the windows. They were locked, too, and boarded up on the inside. Next, she searched Claude's room for a key. Finding none, she informed Homer that she was going to break into the furnace room with an axe.

"Mother, you are not to do anything foolish," Homer said.

Mrs. Bigelow began to seethe with rage and frustration. "And what do *you* intend doing, might I ask?"

"Nothing."

"Nothing? You intend to sit there doing nothing when, for all you know, our very lives are threatened? It's about what I'd expect of you. It's no wonder Claude has got the upper hand. It's no wonder he acts as if he were lord of the manor and we mere peasants. He knows you wouldn't say boo to a rabbit. He knows you haven't got the courage to stand up to him, no matter what he does. Well, I intend to find out what he's doing in the furnace room. I'm going to break the door down."

"What *good* would it do?"

"I'd find out what he's up to."

"I know what he's up to—at least, I think I do. He's making counterfeit money."

"Making counterfeit money—is that all? Well, I'm certainly glad to hear he's found such an innocent pastime. Naturally nobody would object to him doing that."

"Listen to reason, Mother. Supposing I were to go to Claude and say, 'Now, look here, you've got to stop making money in the cellar.' He'd laugh in my face and keep right on making it. And what could I do about it? Could I go to the police? You know I couldn't, and you know why," Homer answered himself. "So for all I care, Claude can print enough money to keep him in Cadillacs for the rest of his life. *I* don't know what he's doing, so if he's ever caught, nobody can accuse me of being an accomplice. All I hope is that he'll take the stuff and get the hell out of here one of these days. He will, you know. He won't be satisfied for long with this kind of living. He's getting restless already. . . . I don't *want* to know what he's doing in the furnace room. I figure the smart thing is not to go snooping."

"Well. . . ." Mrs. Bigelow had to admit that Homer's reasoning made sense.

"So let's forget about it, shall we?"

That's easier said than done, Mrs. Bigelow thought as she sat in the rose arbor waiting for George, wondering how she could put him off without hurting his feelings, and without making him lose hope, too. She had never expected to receive a proposal of marriage, at her age, and the wonder of it almost bowled her over. But how could she go off and leave Dolly, with that criminal in the house, turning their lives all topsy-turvy, demanding money, plotting heaven knew what? She could not even consider her own happiness until they had got rid of him and Dolly was safe.

George called for her on the dot of eight, as he had promised. They drove through the village, over the hills beyond, and stopped at last in a leaf-shaded lovers' lane which at this hour was deserted except for them.

"Have you thought it over?" George asked. It had not occurred to him, before, that a woman would have to *think* about a proposal of marriage from him. He did not believe it now. He thought Mrs. Bigelow was merely being feminine. Women, he knew, were expected to display indecision at such a time, to pretend that the idea of marriage was so new to them it required consideration. He was willing to wait, but not too long.

"What I thought we'd do tomorrow," he went on, "is spend the whole day in town. Buy the license first thing, then you'd help me pick out a ring, and we'd spend the afternoon buying your trousseau. Would you like that?"

"Oh, George . . . !" She almost burst into tears.

"Don't you 'Oh, George' me! I'm going to keep on asking until you say yes. That excuse about not being able to leave Dolly and Homer is all nonsense and you know it. . . . Maybe you don't like me," he suggested. He tried to look anxious, but the absurdity of such an idea made him laugh. He had never been troubled with misgivings about himself, had always taken it for granted that people liked him.

"You know it's not that!"

"I'm getting sick and tired of living with Fred and Lola. 'At your age,' they keep saying, as if I was a thousand years old. As a matter of fact, I've got more pep than the two of them put together. They're a couple of stick-in-the-muds."

"Young people are all like that nowadays. They've got no spirit of adventure. They're afraid to try anything new."

"They're a dull lot," George agreed.

"Yes, they are. And what's more, they like being dull. They want to be in a rut. They call it security." Mrs. Bigelow remembered that her own life—up to now—had been as unexciting as anyone's, but the difference was, she told herself, that she hadn't been satisfied. "When Homer came into his money I suggested renting a villa in the south of France, or perhaps in Rome—one of those old castles; I've seen pictures of them—where we could mingle with movie stars and take a look at the way the

other half lives, but they said, 'Oh, dear, the expense!'
and 'Would it be worth while?' What they really want is a
money-back guarantee on everything."

"Why don't we go there?"

"Where?"

"Rome. Any place."

"It would be nice." Mrs. Bigelow sighed deeply.

"What I'd like to do is not say a word to anyone beforehand, then send a wire to Fred and Lola saying we're on
our honeymoon. I can just see their faces. Shall we do
that?"

"I'll have to think about it." Mrs. Bigelow turned her
head to wipe away a tear.

In the middle of the night, as she sat sleepless beside her
open window, catching the blossom-scented breeze, she
thought she was more unhappy than she had been at
seventeen, when she fell in love for the first time. Tears
slanted down her face, and she did not realize it was
frustration, not a broken heart, that made her cry. She
could not keep putting George off forever. He might
get tired of waiting. He might find someone else, someone younger. . . . She pictured him sprinting up the gang-
plank of a ship bound for the Orient, carrying—as in a
cartoon—a gay young woman under one arm and a
suitcase under the other.

It's all Homer's fault, she thought, counting over his
shortcomings like a rosary: too weak-kneed to stand up
for his own rights, not enough gumption to protect his
own family, allowing his black-sheep relatives to ruin
his wife's happiness. His mother-in-law's happiness,
too. . . . He is ruining my life, Mrs. Bigelow told herself,
mopping her tears with the skirt of her nightgown. My
last chance at happiness!

Chapter Six

"**D**AVE and I would love a week end in the country," Muriel said to Grace as they left the hairdresser's.

"It's too bad our place is so small; we would love to have you otherwise." Grace's voice lacked sincerity, Muriel thought.

"We could tuck in anywhere," she said.

Grace paused before a shop window to examine her reflection. She patted her new sleek coiffure. "Shall we try on a few dresses before lunch?"

They tried on half a dozen each, taking their time. A middle-aged saleswoman with swollen ankles fussed in and out of the fitting room, bringing dresses from the racks outside, taking away those they had discarded as unsuitable, offering advice and compliments.

"I'll take this one," Grace said at last.

"I had no idea you intended to *buy* anything," Muriel said in a cross voice when the saleswoman had taken the dress away to be boxed. "I thought we were only looking."

When they were eating lunch, she said, "All this refurbishing we're going in for—new clothes, new hairdos —I presume it's to impress someone."

"Not necessarily. I simply realized that I had been letting myself go."

"If you don't want Dave for the week end, I could come by myself. I would rather leave him at home, anyway."

"I don't know where you would sleep."

"You must have a couch. Perhaps your sister would let me sleep at her house." Muriel waited a moment, then said petulantly, "You *know* I'm dying to meet this fascinating writer. Why be so selfish about him? We've always shared things."

"I don't know what you mean." Grace pushed aside the remains of her low-calorie salad. "He is my sister's guest, not mine. The only time I see him is when I go to Dolly's house."

"I don't care whose house I meet him in. I simply want to meet him."

"Well, then, come next week end, if you want to. But won't Dave mind being left alone?"

"He'll hate it," Muriel said with satisfaction.

"Mightn't he become bored, and get into mischief?"

"I don't care if he does. It would be a relief, in a way. It would leave me free to develop my personality and make myself attractive in case I meet someone else. Shall I come on Saturday, then?"

"All right." Grace glanced at her watch, then gathered up her handbag and gloves. "I must hurry."

"You're not catching the early train?"

"Yes."

"But you always take the late one."

"I've finished my shopping. There's no need to stay longer."

"And you might miss something at home. Well, run along to your Mr. Richards, then, and captivate him with your new coiffure and your new clothes. It's nice that someone has something to look forward to."

Eloise had the house to herself, except for Mr. Richards, who was dozing on the terrace. Homer and Dolly and Mrs. Bigelow had gone off somewhere right after lunch, saying they would not be home until dinner time. Mr. Newby was setting out annuals in the beds along the driveway. Beyond the hedge the handsome young gardener from next door was also setting out annuals. Eloise barely glanced his way. She had given *him* up long ago. During her first weeks at Dove Cottage, when she had caught sight of him working near the hedge, she had made excuses to go into the garden, hoping to become better acquainted with him. He had answered her wave with a polite nod and kept on working. When she had tried to break the ice with a few sociable remarks he had done nothing but blush and stammer. One evening she saw him eating sandwiches and coffee in the village drug store. She had seated herself on the next stool and in a casual friendly way tried to engage him in conversation. He had been practically tongue-tied, and so respectful that she had concluded it would be a waste of time to cultivate him. He had not once glanced at her figure. Mr. Richards, on the other hand, glanced at her figure a great deal. Whenever she entered a room where he was his eyes went u-p and d-o-w-n. This was so gratifying that she had squandered a whole week's salary on a low-necked form-fitting jersey sweater in a pale lime-green color which the salesgirl had assured her went beautifully with her dark eyes. She was wearing this today.

Before she abandoned her afternoon chores and went upstairs to fix her face and borrow some of Mrs. Bigelow's rose perfume, she made sure that Mr. Richards was still on the terrace. He was lying back with his eyes closed. She had heard him say, earlier, that he intended to spend the afternoon there, resting after his busy morning. Nowadays he spent every morning in his hobby room in the cellar, working behind the locked door. He had told Eloise, in the confiding, half-joking voice he used when they were alone, that he was working on something which would make him absolutely irresistible to women. Laugh! She had giggled for an hour. As if he wasn't that already.

Through an upstairs window she saw Raymond leave the gardener's cottage and limp slowly off across the fields towards the village. So that left the two of them completely alone: herself and Mr. Richards. Mr. Newby, being old and pottery, did not count. Eloise knew that Grace was spending the day in town, and she thanked God for that. Grace was rather inclined to throw herself at Mr. Richards, she thought; always hanging around, dropping in every afternoon, sitting on a low footstool on the terrace, looking up at him while he talked. A person would think she didn't have a husband of her own. But—and Eloise had to laugh every time she thought of this—only yesterday, when Grace had been sitting there gazing up at him, making her eyes big, flattering him with her rapt attention, Eloise had gone out to see if there was anything they wanted; and what had Mr. Richards done, on the sly, but pinch her, Eloise, on the behind. She had pretended to be shocked, of course, had given him a good haughty glare, but it hadn't fooled him. As she was going through the door he had turned around, away from Grace, and lowered one eyelid in the most roguish and meaningful wink.

Thinking about this, Eloise gave herself a final reckless spray of perfume, twirled before the long mirror, smoothed her eyebrows with a moistened fore-finger, admired her red mouth, then went downstairs. He was still on the terrace. She would make a nice gin cocktail— he had taught her how to make all kinds of drinks, joking about how she could get a job as a bartender any day— and take it out to him.

She was putting in the lemon peel when Pink's delivery truck drove up to the back door, with Jack Turner at the wheel. "Oh, God!" Eloise said aloud in a tragic voice. She had forgotten they had ordered groceries that morning.

Jack staggered into the kitchen and dumped his load of groceries on the table. "You alone?" he asked, not quite looking at Eloise. "I thought I saw them in the village. Why didn't they take the new car?"

"He doesn't like it."

"What'd he buy it for, then?"

Eloise shrugged. "I never ask why they do things. Anyway, it's not his. It belongs to Mr. Richards."

"They tell you that?"

"No."

"How do you know who it belongs to, then?"

"Mr. Richards is the only one who ever uses it."

"Well, I happen to know for a fact that Mr. Flynn paid for it, anyway. I heard Bert Smith in the bank telling Mr. Pink." Jack leaned against the drainboard and gazed out. "Say, that's some buggy! Boy, what I'd give for a buggy like that!"

Go. *Go*. Eloise prayed silently.

Jack pulled up a chair and straddled it, his arms folded along the top. "Why'n't you relax? I thought you said they were out."

"Mr. Richards is in."

"Say, I saw him yesterday, driving the new car. All

done up in dark glasses, like a celebrity trying to be incognito." Jack stressed the third syllable.

"He is a celebrity."

Jack tossed a bag of humbugs on the table. "Something for you," he said. "Don't I even get a piece of cake?"

Eloise set out a plate of iced cupcakes. "But you'll have to hurry," she warned. "I'm away behind in my work."

"They'll never know the difference." He devoured a cupcake in one bite. "Sweep the dirt under the carpet. That's what my mother does. What's this?" He picked up the gin cocktail.

"It's a drink for Mr. Richards."

Jack stuck his nose in the glass and sniffed. "Gin," he pronounced, airing his knowledge. "What else is in it?"

"Lemon peel and stuff."

"Whyn't you make me one?"

"I'm too busy."

"Give me a taste, anyway."

Eloise snatched the glass from him. "This is for Mr. Richards. And you'll have to go."

"I can't say I approve of you being here alone with him." Jack was beginning to suspect he was not welcome. "And you want to know something else? That sweater's too tight."

"It's the size I always wear."

"Furthermore, I think you're wearing falsies."

"I am not!"

"Don't you go hanging around that Mr. Richards, with that sweater on. I don't like the look of him."

"He's a perfect gentleman."

"He's old enough to be your father, too, but I wouldn't trust him not to make a pass at you; not with that sweater on."

"If you were a gentleman you wouldn't go making remarks about people's figures."

"Some figure!" He threw a glance at it, then looked quickly down at the cake he was finishing. "You want to go to the movies tonight?"

"If you like."

"You want to go, or don't you?"

"All right."

"Nobody's forcing you. If you'd rather stay at home, all you've got to do is say so."

"I said I'd go, didn't I?"

"Seven-thirty, then?"

"All right." But for heaven's sake, *go*! she willed him, holding the door open.

Though unable to read her mind, Jack could not mistake her action. "I'm going, I'm *going*!" He snatched another cake from the table. "Some welcome!" he grumbled.

Halfway back to the village, he decided that Eloise's excuse about being behind with her work was too flimsy to hold water. So why had she pushed him out? So she could be alone with that Mr. Richards? As his jealousy mounted, Eloise's desirability mounted, too. "I ought to bust that old geezer right in the nose," he muttered.

The gin cocktail was ruined, the ice all melted. Glancing at the clock as she made up another, Eloise noted with irritation that it was three-thirty already. By four-thirty at the latest she would have to begin washing up the luncheon dishes, which were still piled in the sink. In her haste, she slopped too much gin into the glass. Never mind, he would not complain about that. He would say, "Won't you have one, too?" and of course she would have to say no, but she might take a sip of his if he offered it. If he said, "What are you doing tonight?" she would say she wasn't doing a thing. Even if he didn't ask her, she might work it into the conversation that her evenings were all free.

She placed the glass on a tray and walked through the study. When she opened the door leading to the terrace she actually felt her heart leap with rage. For there was Grace sitting on the steps with her hat in her hand, looking up at Mr. Richards, making her eyes big, smiling her silly smile.

Eloise turned quickly and walked back to the kitchen. So great was her disappointment, and her hatred for Grace, that tears filled her eyes. She drank the gin cocktail herself, hoping it would make her drunk. It only made her sick. After dinner, purged but still heavy-headed, she sat in her aunt's house waiting for Jack and another routine evening at the movies.

Before she reached the village station, Grace had given herself a reason for catching the early train. She must hurry home to see how Raymond was. When she left the house that morning he had been lying in bed giving little moans of pain, having awakened with one of his headaches.

"Would you like me to stay at home?" she had asked at the last minute. She was dressed and ready, her train was leaving in ten minutes, and the village taxi was waiting at the door.

He lay back with a wet towel over his eyes. "I don't want to upset your plans."

"I suppose I could cancel my appointment."

He moved his head from side to side, groaning.

"But I may not get another appointment for days."

"Oh, for God's sake, go!" he cried in a suffering voice.

"Shall I leave the coffee pot on?"

He doubled up as if retching. After a minute he lifted the towel from his eyes to see if she really meant to leave him alone. When he saw that she did, he lay back again, limp, exhausted, reproaching her with his martyrdom. He then asked for aspirin, for ice, for his bedding to be arranged more comfortably. He found a dozen little jobs for her to do before she went, implying that none of them could really help, that only a miracle could alleviate his suffering. She had almost missed her train.

As the train neared the village, she stared out at the flying landscape, wondering how she could prevent Muriel from coming out for the week end. Another time, she would have welcomed company. Earlier in the season, looking forward to the novelty of country living, she had pictured herself being hostess to a party of friends every week end. (No worries, then, about where they would sleep; they could tuck in anywhere, as Muriel had reminded.)

If Raymond's headache is no better, she thought, I can telephone Muriel and tell her not to come. Or I could develop some indisposition myself. But someone else's indispositions would not keep Muriel away. Not when she was dying of curiosity.

Grace could blame no one but herself for Muriel's curiosity, since she had unwisely talked too much about Claude during the first weeks of his visit. What disturbed her now was that she had given Muriel a false impression of him. She had stressed his good points—his charm, his wit, his good looks—and had avoided mentioning his bad ones. Muriel, when she came for the week end would say, "But you didn't tell me he was *that* kind," and Grace would know better than to ask what she meant. One glance into his eyes, and Muriel would feel called upon to give hackneyed advice about moths and flames and singed wings.

Grace was beginning to wonder other things about Claude. His writing, for instance, and his reason for being at Dove Cottage. He had turned out to be so unlike Homer that she could not imagine them being bosom friends, even childhood bosom friends. Still, people do change, she thought. Perhaps when they were young they had been more alike. Perhaps a different environment had turned Homer into a quiet homebody, given Claude his bantering man-of-the-world air.

As for his writing, Grace had given up asking about that, since she never received a satisfactory reply. "Has *anybody* read any of his books?" she had asked Dolly one day. Her mother answered, in a voice that could be meant to convey anything from sarcasm to kindly counsel: "Don't show your ignorance by admitting that *you* haven't read them."

At the station, she thought that if she were not in such a hurry to get back to Raymond, it might be nice to walk home through the fields on such a day, but she was wearing high heels, and the village taxi was idling nearby, the driver eyeing her expectantly. When she moved forward, he hopped out and opened the door.

As they turned into Main Street, both she and the driver caught sight of Raymond looking in a shop window. Grace leaned forward and half raised her hand, then, as Raymond did not turn, sank back into the seat. "You want to pick him up?" the driver asked over his shoulder.

"No." Grace put her hand up to shield her face in case Raymond did turn. When the driver failed to pick up speed quickly she said in a sharp voice, "Drive on, please."

Farther along, past the shops, a number of cars were parked in front of the community recreation center. Grace spotted Homer's black sedan. "What is going on?" she asked the driver.

"Flower show or something. Mr. and Mrs. Flynn are in there, and your mother. I noticed them when I drove a couple of the garden club ladies over. You want to stop?"

"No, I'll go straight home. And hurry, please." Grace was suddenly frantic to be at home. She took a compact from her handbag and touched up her face. Not once did she glance out at the flowering landscape.

Halfway up the separate lane that led to the gardener's cottage, she caught sight of Claude on the terrace. "I'll get out here," she told the driver. She paid him off, threw her parcels behind some bushes, then, slowly, as if she had not been hurrying at all, she sauntered toward the terrace, pausing to break off, first, a spray of honeysuckle, then a cluster of Dorothy Perkins rosebuds. She moved toward her goal with a dreamy abstracted air, sniffing her fragrant bouquet.

"Hello, there!" Claude smiled lazily from his reclining position.

"Oh . . . !" Grace looked up. "I didn't see you."

"I wondered where you were." He pushed himself up a few inches and stuffed another cushion under his shoulders. "Everybody seems to have deserted me."

"Isn't Dolly here?" Grace paused on the step and took off her hat. "I really stopped by to see her."

"I'm all by my little lonesome."

"Where is everybody?"

"Does it matter? I'm here; and now that you've come, I don't care if the others ever show up." Claude stretched out a languid hand and pulled another chair up close to

122

his own. "Come and sit down," he invited, patting the seat.

Grace sat on the step, instead.

"Now, tell me where you've been and what you've been up to. You've had your hair done, I can see that. V-e-r-y becoming." He half-closed his eyes, nodding. "What else have you been doing?"

"I had lunch with a girl friend in the city."

"What did you talk about?" He looked at her engagingly, his head on one side. "Did you talk about me?"

"She knows you're staying here, of course."

"I wonder what you told her about me," he said with captivating candor. "Tell me, now!" he coaxed. "Do you think she got the impression that I'm someone nice to know?"

"She's coming out for the week end expressly to see you." Grace laughed, then added. "She'll be bored, of course. Oh, not with you!—but there's so little to do in the country."

"It is deadly, isn't it? I've often wondered what *you* do with yourself. You're not the country type."

"I fritter away my time."

"We're birds of a feather," Claude murmured.

"You can't find it so dull, surely, or you wouldn't stay."

"The trouble with me is, I just can't bear to hurt people," Claude said earnestly. "I hadn't seen Homer for years, you know, until that night I dropped in for a visit and he insisted—they all insisted—that I stay here with them. I'd been under the weather, you see, and Homer said, 'Of course you'll stay with us. We won't hear of you staying at a hotel.' So I thought, well, if it gives them pleasure, then I *would* stay. Homer and Dolly are so sweet. I just love them. Your mother, too. I do think she's wonderful. . . . I pretend to love it here for their sakes. They'd be so hurt if they thought—oh, you mustn't tell them!"

"Of course not."

"You do promise?"

"Yes."

"I knew you'd understand," Claude said with a grateful smile. "You see, we *are* birds of a feather."

"How long since you'd seen Homer?" Grace asked.

"Oh, years and years."

"Had you kept in touch; written letters?"

"Off and on." Claude threw his feet over the side of the chaise longue and sat up. He lit two cigarettes and handed one to Grace. "But we grew up together, so that made a difference. I always looked on him as a sort of older brother."

"It's funny he never spoke of you, but then he doesn't speak much of his early life. I don't think he likes to remember his childhood. Did you know his aunt, the one who left him the money?"

Claude considered this. "Let's say we were slightly acquainted. Did you know her?"

"I'd forgotten he had an aunt, until he got word of his inheritance. I'm not sure that Homer was too fond of her. What was she like?"

"She was a horrible old baggage. No, really, I mean it!" He laughed. "Sagging jowls, rusty, musty clothes, always chewing peppermints. . . . But let's not talk about her. Let's talk about us."

"I've been meaning to ask you about your books," Grace said. "I haven't been able to buy one anywhere. The bookstores don't seem to carry them at all."

"Those old books. Honestly, I get so embarrassed!" He

reached for her hand and pulled her up to stand beside him. "Let's walk in the garden. . . . Oh, you've had your nails done!" He turned her hand in his and stroked her fingers. "Little pink shells."

When she did not withdraw her hand he tucked it under his arm and led her down the garden path. She felt him watching her face, waiting to see how she was going to behave. She was not sure, herself. It would depend on how he behaved.

At the far end of the garden, out of sight of the house, he sat down on a stone bench and pulled her down beside him. She thought he was going to put his arms around her, and tensed herself to protest. Instead, he sat staring in front of him, holding her hand loosely, as if it were some object he had picked up and forgotten.

Vexed, she drew away from him and said, "How do you mean, embarrassed?"

"Well, in the first place, I nearly fell over when Lola Adams said she'd read those old books of mine. I thought everybody had forgotten them, I wrote them such years ago."

"Are they out of print now?"

"Out of print and forgotten." He reclaimed her hand. "They weren't even popular when they were *in* print. I don't suppose more than a handful of people ever read them. I don't know why I didn't say so, then and there —the day Lola said she'd read them, I mean—but the fact is, I got such a kick out of being hailed as a celebrity. . . . And I didn't like to offend Lola, because, between you and me, I doubt if she's ever read *Pacific Paradise* or anything else I ever wrote. She was just saying that. . . . And then, later, I was afraid *you'd* be disappointed if I confessed that I wasn't truly famous. Are you disappointed?"

Grace shook her head. It made no difference whatso-
ever to her. She was much more interested in what Claude
was doing than in what he was saying, for he had rested
one arm on the back of the seat and was playing with her
pearl necklace. His fingers crept softly around her neck
as he touched each bead.

"Do you like me a little bit, even though I'm not a
celebrity?" His hand slid under her dress and rested in
the hollow of her shoulder. He leaned forward and
kissed her.

"You mustn't . . ." she whispered.

"I can't help myself." He ran his other hand up her
arm and kissed her again. "I've been wanting to do that
since the minute I met you."

"Someone will see us."

He looked around. "Could we go in there?" he asked,
indicating a tool shed against the fence.

In the earthy warmth of the little shed he closed the
door, shutting out the light, then turned and took her in
his arms.

Chapter Seven

ONE wet afternoon in late June Homer drove to the village to buy bone meal for his tuberous begonias. Dolly and her mother remained at home, Dolly from choice, since she disliked being out in the rain, Mrs. Bigelow because she had nowhere to go. Earlier in the day, before the rain set in, she had gone painting, but alone, for George had grown tired of being put off. He was losing heart, beginning to wonder if there was something wrong with him. Each time he read a magazine advertisement about people who, for one reason or another, were not socially acceptable, he wondered if he possessed the undesirable disorder. He bought so many gargles, deodorants and tonics that he smelled, Lola complained, like a walking drug store. He spent whole days by himself, brooding, trying to figure out why his proposal had not been accepted.

Since Claude was absent—and he was absent a good deal lately, going out more in the afternoons—Dolly and Mrs. Bigelow were enjoying a peaceful cup of tea in the living room when Homer returned from the village. Soon afterwards Raymond dropped in, looking out of sorts.

"Where is Grace?" Dolly asked him. "We never see her nowadays."

"You're not the only one," Raymond answered morosely. "She's never at home any more."

Homer gave him a peculiar look. "Where does she go?"

"To the city, to see that friend of hers, Muriel. They go shopping."

"Every day?"

"Almost every day. Sometimes she stays and has dinner with Muriel, then they go to the movies. I thought we came out here to rest," Raymond complained. "I can't say I admire that Muriel. When she came out for the week end she talked about her husband as if he were someone she was forced to put up with—a poor relation or somebody."

"They could hardly go shopping every day," Homer said.

"You mean you have to prepare your own dinner, you poor thing?"

"Grace leaves a cold supper for me. I haven't much appetite."

Homer fidgeted about the room. "Is she with Muriel today?" he asked, staring out at the slackening rain.

"I suppose so. I didn't ask her."

"You must stay and have dinner with us," Dolly said.

Homer turned from the window. "Is Grace not coming home for dinner tonight?"

"She didn't say she wouldn't be home." Raymond helped himself to a piece of cake and bit into it with a gloomy air, as if he were forcing himself to eat.

He left half an hour later.

"Will you for heaven's sake stop fidgeting?" Mrs. Bigelow said, exasperated, as Homer continued to wander about the room. "You're giving me the willies."

He stopped his prowling abruptly and faced them. "Grace is *not* with Muriel today," he said.

"Where is she, then?"

Homer went into the hall to make sure the kitchen door was closed before he began his story, then, to be on the safe side, closed the living room door as well. "They didn't have any bone meal at the hardware store in the village," he began, "so I thought, well, it will only take ten minutes to run over to Greenwood and get some. Frank Gates rode with me. He'd had a call from the Greenwood police about some counterfeit money that had turned up at the bank there."

"Oh, no . . . !"

"Oh, yes! He told me about it on the way over. I questioned him rather carefully about it—did they have any clue as to where the money came from, and so on. I hope he didn't think I was showing too much interest. It was a twenty-dollar American bill, he said, a very good imitation of the real thing, but bearing the same serial number as one that turned up in the local bank last week. He was rather evasive about telling me whether they had any clues as to the counterfeiter's identity."

"Claude would never be so rash . . . !" Dolly pressed her hands to her face. "Does Frank suspect him, do you think?"

"I don't know. He did mention Claude—not in connection with the money, though it seemed to me he looked at me in a peculiar way. All he said was, 'Is Mr. Richards still with you?' in a kind of conversational way, but I thought he *looked* funny when he said it. I may be imagining things."

"We're all jumping to conclusions." Dolly tried to sound as if she believed this. "There's no reason to suppose that Claude . . . We don't really know what he's doing in the cellar."

"He'll land us all in jail before he's finished," Mrs.

Bigelow predicted. "If I were you, Homer, I'd do something."

"I keep hoping that something will happen," Homer said, staring into the garden. The rain had stopped, but the trees still sighed, scattering wet leaves. The roses looked drowned.

"Something will happen, all right!" Mrs. Bigelow nodded grimly. "I think we can depend on that. But I don't see what all this has got to do with Grace."

"On the way back from Greenwood we stopped at that place on the highway, the Red Hen. It's a sort of tavern. Frank wanted to have a beer, so I thought I might as well have one, too. . . ."

"Well, go *on*!"

"We were sitting at the bar, and Frank said, 'Homer, isn't that your sister-in-law and Mr. Richards?' I turned around and there they were, in a corner booth, with their backs to us. Then the bartender spoke up and said they were regular customers—came in every day or so."

"Did you speak to them?"

"I don't know why I didn't. They were so busy talking they didn't see us, and I was trying to act nonchalant, I guess—as if I wasn't surprised to see them. . . . As if we haven't got enough troubles, Grace has to go running around with *him*!"

Mrs. Bigelow bridled at this. "I don't see anything at all unusual in their being together," she said. "If Grace happened to be waiting at the station for a taxi, and if Claude happened along, why wouldn't he offer her a lift home? Then, when they passed the Red Hen, he might have suggested dropping in there for a drink. Or she might have. What's so unusual about that? You must remember that Grace has been led to believe that Claude is a respectable person, a dear friend of yours, Homer.

You have gone to great lengths to convince her of that."

"The Red Hen is on the other side of the village."

"I *know* where it is." Mrs. Bigelow had been there with George one sunny afternoon—years ago, it seemed to her now, though it was less than two months ago, before Claude came.

"If they just happened to drop in, why did he have his car parked away around at the back, as if he didn't want anyone to see it? And why did the bartender say they were regular customers? 'Every day or so,' he said."

"But surely Grace wouldn't do anything so foolish!" Seeking reassurance, Dolly looked appealingly from her mother to Homer.

"Grace has been properly brought up," her mother answered sharply, and gave Homer a good glare. She had become, lately, more short-tempered than ever with him, since because of him she was lonely and unwed. "Furthermore, she has a perfectly good husband. It just so happens that she had been taught to be agreeable to people whom she had been led to believe are trusted family friends."

"Well, it certainly looked funny," Homer said.

"What looks funnier to me is my daughter's husband harboring a criminal."

Homer sighed despondently. "I just don't know what to do."

"It's high time you found out, then," his mother-in-law said. She rose and brushed the crumbs from her skirt. "I'm going upstairs. But don't go casting aspersions at innocent people," she warned from the doorway.

Dolly threw open the window, for the sun had broken through the clouds and lay in glistening patches on the dripping leaves. Robins hopped on the lawn, and a great spike of blue delphinium lay across the petunia border. "Perhaps Mother is right," she said, trying to sound hopeful.

Homer did not think so, but he felt too apathetic to protest. "I gave Mr. Newby his notice this morning," he said.

"But you can't do all the gardening yourself!"

"We can get an odd-jobs man in once in a while to clean up."

"Your lovely garden!" Dolly mourned. "Then we'll let Eloise go, too," she decided. "We don't really need her," she went on quickly as Homer began to expostulate. "I have so little to do that I am becoming bored. I think I was happier when I was busy." She clasped her hands together and stared at the rosy nails, the smooth knuckles, as if she were just realizing how they had changed since she had stopped doing her own housework. "Are things really that bad?" she asked.

"If Claude keeps on demanding money the way he is, we may have to let the house go, too. We're living away beyond our income. It will only be a matter of time until our capital is gone." Homer added after a long pause, "Sometimes I wish I were back at the bank."

"Oh, Homer, no!" Dolly pressed her cheek to his and covered his eyes, as if she could protect him from such thoughts.

Mrs. Bigelow was not so certain of Grace's innocence as she had pretended to be. She felt relief, therefore, when Claude showed up for dinner.

"You'll speak to him about this afternoon, of course," she said to Homer. "About his being at the Red Hen with Grace, I mean."

"Of course," Homer agreed, but he was so long doing

it that she tried to prod him into action by bringing up the subject herself.

"Have you seen Grace recently?" she asked Claude in what she thought was a deceptively careless tone, as they were all finishing their coffee on the terrace.

He looked up, about to shake his head, then, seeing her expression, gave her a disarming smile. "It's funny you should ask that, because I happened to run into her this very afternoon, in the village."

"Oh, really?" Mrs. Bigelow so overdid her nonchalance that he knew she was trying to trap him. "You drove her home, I suppose?"

"As a matter of fact, no. She had some shopping to do, she said. I did take her to that charming little tavern for a drink, though. The Red Hen, I believe it's called. Then I drove her back to the village and dropped her off at the supermarket. I believe she took a taxi home." He added in his most friendly voice, "You must let me take you there one day, Auntie. To the Red Hen, I mean—not the supermarket. A quaint little place. Would you like that?"

"No, thank you," she said, glaring at Homer, trying to make him take over from there.

"Your poor nerves," Claude said with a fond smile. "You're all upset these days. Is it because George doesn't come to see you as often as he used to? I think it's just a dirty shame, Auntie, the way he's treating you."

This remark, plus Homer's do-nothing attitude, so infuriated Mrs. Bigelow that she was unable to speak for a moment.

"Someone coming?" Homer, on the alert for any diversion, was the first to hear tires crunching on the drive.

It was Frank Gates. "Just happened to be passing," he said. "Thought I'd drop in and look at your garden, Homer." He accepted the cup of coffee Dolly poured for him and sat down.

"This is Mr. Richards, Frank. I don't believe you've met."

"I've seen Mr. Richards in the village." Frank heaved himself to his feet again. "Glad to know you, Mr. Richards," he said heartily, looking Claude over as they shook hands. "It's not often we have a famous writer in our midst."

"I'd hardly call myself famous." Claude looked modestly aside.

"Been under the weather, I hear."

"Yes." Claude assumed his most invalidish expression.

"Nothing like good country air."

"That's right."

"Mr. Gates is the village police chief," Mrs. Bigelow told Claude.

"Interesting. . . ." He helped himself to a cigarette, then passed the box to Frank.

"Did you catch that counterfeiter yet, Mr. Gates?" Mrs. Bigelow gazed intently at Claude. He never batted an eye. "Did you know there's a counterfeiter at large, palming phoney money off on the village shopkeepers?" she asked, still watching him, trying to see behind his bland mask.

"You're joking, Auntie!" He smiled, half chiding, half incredulous. "In this sleepy little place? It's hard to believe."

"Mr. Gates is looking for him," she went on. "Have you any idea who did it, Mr. Gates?"

"We'll find him, don't you worry." Frank set down his empty cup. "Now, what say we have a look at that garden of yours, Homer?" He winked at Dolly. "I've been hearing so much about Homer's garden—to hear him talk you'd think there wasn't another garden in the country that could touch it; roses big as soup bowls, he claims—that I said to the boys, 'I'll just take a look and see for myself.' " He gave Homer a friendly slap on the shoulder as they went down the steps together. "I'll see you again, Mr. Richards." He turned to Claude with what Mrs. Bigelow imagined was a meaningful glance. "How's the old book coming along, Homer?" he was asking as they strolled out of sight.

Claude looked at his watch, yawned, and rose to his feet. "Well, I'm off, girls." He filled his cigarette case from the box on the table. "Don't wait up for me."

As soon as the door slammed behind him, Mrs. Bigelow also stirred herself.

"Where are you going, Mother?" Dolly asked.

"I'm going to see what Grace is up to, that's where. It's just occurred to me that we've seen very little of her these past weeks. She used to come here sometimes in the evenings; now she never does."

"I'll go with you," Dolly said.

The garden sparkled with late yellow sunshine. The air was clear as glass and all the birds were singing. Butterflies drifted over the flower beds, small coppers and blues, red admirals and painted ladies, hovering and settling with drowsy indolence. When she had lived in the city flat Dolly had dreamed of evenings such as this, had pictured herself and Homer sitting hand in hand through the perfumed twilight absorbing the lovely peace of summer. Now anxiety so clouded her mind that she could feel nothing but sadness.

At the gardener's cottage Raymond was lying on the

living room couch nursing a bandaged wrist. The dinner dishes were still piled in the kitchen sink.

In her bedroom, where she was dressing to go out, Grace said, "Oh, damn!" as she fished for a broken shoulder strap. This was just another in a series of frustrating incidents which had occurred to delay her. She had promised to meet Claude in the village at eight o'clock. Then Raymond had complained of indigestion, and while he was mixing up bicarbonate of soda, had broken a glass and cut his wrist. It was not a deep cut, and she had persuaded him that he did not need a doctor, but it was some time before she got the wrist bandaged to his satisfaction. Then, in her haste to get dressed, she had ripped an underarm seam, and finally broken the shoulder strap, which she now fastened with a safety pin.

These were minor irritations, but they reflected the deeper disorganization which love had caused. She had had so little practice that the strain of carrying on an affair—the struggle to invent and then remember excuses for being where she should not be, the fear that she might not be able to keep up with her own deception, the constant hurrying to keep appointments, and above all the effort of pretending that Claude was worthy of her love —was becoming so burdensome that she sometimes wondered why clandestine affairs were always presented so attractively in books. She was tired, too. All the running about had made her lose pounds. She imagined that the attitude of other people had changed, but this was really her own fear of being found out, for she was not nearly as careless of the world's opinion as she thought she was. Even the deep envy of Muriel, whom she was forced to use as a confidante and an excuse to be away from home, had lost its appeal.

There was no end in sight, that was the trouble. If she were to lose Claude, not to another woman, of course, but in some less painful way—if he went back to Africa, for instance, and there was devoured by lions—she would enjoy her heartbreak and be at peace, having something to look back on, memories to sort over as proof that she had once been desired. She did not realize this, however, and her only wish, this evening, was to meet Claude in the village.

Seeing her mother and sister walking through the garden, looming along the flagged walk with the set faces of people about to undertake an unpleasant task for another's good, she felt sure they were bent on frustrating her plans.

Since there was no escape, she went into the living room to meet them. "I saw you coming along the path," she said. "You looked like a delegation of suffragettes about to chop down a saloon door. If you could have seen your faces!"

"We merely dropped in for a visit," her mother said.

"I wish you had told me you were coming. I'm going out. I've already called the taxi."

Mrs. Bigelow looked at Dolly, then picked up a magazine and fanned herself with it. "Where are you going?"

"To the village."

"Alone?"

Grace glanced at her husband. "You know Raymond. He never wants to go anywhere."

"Raymond is never asked to go anywhere," he said, holding his bandaged wrist against his chest.

Grace, to avoid being looked at, went to the window and glanced out. Any minute now her taxi would be along. When the silence was prolonged, she had to turn back. "I don't know why you're all looking at me so suspiciously," she complained. "Is there anything wrong with going to the village?"

Her mother answered. "The shops are all closed, so where is there to go?"

"As it happens, I'm going to the dressmaker's."

"Then you won't mind if we go along."

"Surely you can find something more interesting to do."

"Is she any good, this dressmaker?" Dolly asked. "I was thinking I might have some cotton dresses made up. I can never find anything in the stores to fit me."

"No, she's not good," Grace said recklessly. "She's terrible. I would never have gone to her if I had known. Here's my taxi." She snatched her handbag from the table.

"But we're coming, too." Mrs. Bigelow was at her heels as she went out.

"Mother, I would rather go alone if you don't mind."

"Nonsense. Nobody wants to be alone. Come along, Dolly."

"Oh, for heaven's sake!" Grace wrenched open the door of the taxi, brushing aside the driver, who was trying to help. She flung herself into a far corner of the seat. Dolly and Mrs. Bigelow clambered in after her.

"I suppose you think I'm too old to care about clothes," Mrs. Bigelow said, "but if I live to be a hundred, I hope I'll always take pride in my appearance. If this dressmaker is any good, I shall put myself in her hands."

"Mother, I have told you that this woman is not a good dressmaker. She never gets seams straight. You're simply wasting your time, going to her. Besides, I thought I'd sit through a movie afterwards. How will you and Dolly get home? You've come without your handbags."

"We'll go to the movies, too," her mother said, peering

over the driver's shoulder into the rear view mirror as she smoothed her hair. "You can pay our way."

"I'm going with a friend—a girl friend."

"Your friend won't mind. The more the merrier, I always say. . . . But you wouldn't leave poor Raymond alone all evening, would you?"

"Poor Raymond, as you call him, likes his own company. It leaves him free to count over his indispositions. He will tell me all about them when I get back."

Dolly nudged her sister and gave a warning frown. The back of the driver's head seemed to be all ears as he listened to the conversation.

"There's Eloise and the grocer's boy," Dolly said as they drove along the village street. She immediately assumed a worried expression. "I gave that poor child her notice this afternoon. I hope she can find another job."

"Why?" Grace was glad to turn the conversation from herself. "Why did you let her go, I mean?"

"We really don't need her. I found that I was becoming bored with so little to do. She didn't *seem* to mind. . . ." Dolly twisted around in the seat for another look at Eloise and Jack. "But they don't look particularly happy, do they? I suppose they're going to the movies. Eloise is such a nice girl—so young and innocent. I'm glad she has a nice boy like Jack Turner to take her out. No harm can come to her, I feel sure, with such a nice boy . . . Is this the dressmaker's?"

Grace really did have an appointment with the dressmaker, who lived and worked in a flat over a corset shop. The shop window was filled with pink torsos wearing black lace girdles. Through the side door, a flight of steps led to a second-floor hallway. At the back of this hallway, another flight of steps, which Grace had used before, led down to an alley at the rear of the shop, and from there it was but a step through a laneway to the next street, where Claude was waiting.

In the dressmaker's flat, part of the living room had been curtained off to make a waiting room, which was furnished with two chairs, a small table, and a pile of magazines. An unpleasant smell hung in the air, reminders of yesterday's toast and cigarettes. Somewhere in the back a radio was playing popular songs.

"Wait here," Grace said, as she and the dressmaker disappeared behind the curtains.

Unsuspecting, Dolly and Mrs. Bigelow waited for ten minutes. To the blaring of the radio was presently added the whirring of a sewing machine. Mrs. Bigelow rose and peered behind the curtains. The dressmaker was alone, bent over her machine with her mouth full of pins.

Mrs. Bigelow swept the curtains all the way back. The rings clashed along the brass rod. "Where is my daughter?" she demanded, shouting to make herself heard.

The dressmaker whirled around, snatching pins from her mouth. "Lord, you frightened me! I'd forgotten you were there." She switched off the radio. "Mrs. Collins? Why, she was only in for a skirt fitting—over in two minutes. Didn't she tell you? She was meeting a girl friend over on the next street, so she went down the back way. She said you were waiting for someone—your husband, was it, Mrs. Flynn? She asked if I minded—you two ladies waiting out there, I mean, and I said, Lord, *I* didn't mind. Is your husband here now?"

Dolly and Mrs. Bigelow exchanged despairing glances.

"Is anything wrong?" the dressmaker asked, coming forward.

Dolly shook her head. "May I use your telephone?" she asked, trying to keep her voice steady.

"Sure thing. Go ahead."

"This is too much!" Mrs. Bigelow said, as Dolly telephoned Homer. "This is the last straw."

"But you're not certain she's with Claude," Homer said, when Dolly told him how Grace had given them the slip.

"If she were meeting a girl friend, as she said, why was she so anxious to be rid of us?"

"You know Grace," Homer said vaguely. "George was here," he added, turning to his mother-in-law. "He waited for almost an hour."

"Oh, my heavens! What date is it?" Mrs. Bigelow scrabbled through some papers on Homer's desk, searching for a calendar. It was midsummer night, and an amateur theatrical company was staging *A Midsummer Night's Dream* at the Red Barn theater in Lakefield. George had bought tickets for this performance weeks ago.

"How *could* I forget?" she cried. "This is all your fault, Homer," she grumbled as she dialed George's number. "If you had the gumption of a cat you'd do something about that relative of yours. Upsetting our lives, making fools of us all. . . ." Her anger mounted as the telephone at the other end kept ringing and ringing. She imagined it echoing through the empty house.

She tried again ten minutes later. This time Lola answered.

"No, I don't know where Dad is," Lola said. "We just got in, ourselves, so I can't say. . . . He did mention, earlier, that he was going out tonight; to the summer theater at Lakefield, I believe."

"Yes, I know. Are you sure he's not at home? Perhaps in his room . . . ?"

"His car is not here. Shall I ask him to phone you when he does come in?"

"Please do."

"You sound so cross." Lola put on her little-girl voice. "Why is everyone mad at me?"

"I'm sorry. I'm upset."

"Grace and Mr. Richards wouldn't even *speak* to me."

Mrs. Bigelow felt she would die before giving Lola the satisfaction of hearing the obvious question.

Lola answered it, anyway. "It wasn't more than half an hour ago, on the highway. There had been an accident, and a crowd had begun to gather. . . ."

"Grace wasn't hurt?"

"Oh, no. Grace and Mr. Richards had stopped, like everyone else, to see if anyone had been killed. As a matter of fact, the road was blocked, so we were all forced to stop. I saw them at the edge of the crowd, looking on. I waved at them, and tried to push my way toward them, and they simply turned their backs and walked away."

"They didn't see you, I'm sure. Good-bye, Lola."

"Oh, but they did see me. Grace was looking straight at me."

"I'm quite sure she didn't recognize you."

"I don't see how she could help it. I recognized her."

"I must hang up, Lola. Good-bye."

"I'll tell Dad to call you when he comes in. Bye-bye, now."

"Bye-bye, now!" Mrs. Bigelow mimicked in a furious voice as she slammed up the receiver. "Well, it's as we suspected." She turned to Dolly and Homer. "Lola's just informed me that Claude and Grace are stepping out together this evening. She saw them not half an hour ago."

"Where?" Homer stood up.

"Out on the highway. Where are you going?"

"I'm going after them."

"Wait, Homer!" Dolly caught up with him at the door.

"Don't try to stop me, Dolly," he warned.

"You won't do anything foolish, Homer?"

"I'm going to kill him, that's all," Homer said grimly. He was gone before Dolly could stop him. She did not, in fact, try to stop him. It was not until she heard the car starting up, and the crunch of gravel as he turned from the driveway into the street, that she suddenly wondered if he had meant what he said.

"We'll have to stop him, Mother." She began to wring her hands. "You know he loses all reason when he gets worked up. He lets people walk all over him and you think he'll never stand up and fight, then he loses his head and does something foolish."

"Homer? Don't be silly."

"Remember the time he knocked Mr. Williams downstairs?"

"I remember he *said* he knocked Mr. Williams downstairs. If you ask me, I think Mr. Williams fell down by himself. Homer's too cowardly to do anything rash, Dolly. You needn't worry."

"But supposing he does?"

"As far as I'm concerned, if Homer wants to kill Claude, he can go ahead and do it. I wouldn't try to stop him even if I could."

"Oh, Mother!"

"If I was with him, I'd help."

She left Dolly crying in the study and went upstairs, where she sat beside her darkened window waiting for the telephone to ring.

Chapter Eight

ELOISE had known about the affair between Grace and Mr. Richards from the beginning. Being considered on the inside track, she had found her popularity rising among the village women. She would much rather be popular with the village men, but talking about the affair served as an outlet for her own great disappointment, and she made the most of it. She was, in fact, the chief source of information. The village ladies had not realized that a scandal was going on under their noses until Eloise enlightened them.

"From the minute Mr. Richards set foot in the house," she now told anyone who would listen, "she started throwing herself at him. 'Oh, Mr. Richards this. Oh, Mr. Richards that.'" She imitated Grace's throaty voice. "Coming in every afternoon to have cocktails with him, then all of a sudden *not* coming, pretending she had lost interest, trying to throw everyone off the scent. But I knew what they were up to." Eloise spoke with such vehemence that people assumed she knew a great deal more than she actually did.

When she had told all she knew—adding a few frills for good measure—she went home sadly and brooded, feeling unwanted, lacking confidence. Being discarded was disappointing enough, but to be discarded in favor of what in her own mind she termed a middle-aged woman was almost more than Eloise could bear. She had fought gamely to win Mr. Richards' attention—spending a small fortune on cosmetics and perfume at the five-and-ten, going out of her way to be noticed—but nowadays he scarcely glanced her way. Oh, he still winked at her over other people's heads, even pinched her behind when he passed her in the hall, but she realized he did these things from habit, not because it meant anything to him. She had a terrifying vision of herself forever rejected. If she could reach the age of eighteen without anyone wanting to seduce her, she reasoned, she must be singularly lacking in appeal, and might as well resign herself to the bleak prospect of a virginal old age.

Jack Turner, walking her home through the lanes after the movie, reaffirmed that he had known, from the very beginning, that Mr. Richards couldn't be trusted where women were concerned. "He's got a kind of a look in his eye," Jack said. "I'm certainly glad he didn't go chasing after you," he added, taking Eloise's hand.

She snatched her hand away and quickened her step.

"Now what have I said?"

"Nothing."

"All I said was I was glad he didn't go chasing after you."

"You needn't talk as if I was a common strumpet," Eloise said, using one of her mother's words.

"I never said any such thing. I never said you'd *encourage* him."

"I don't know what you think I am."

"I only meant it's a wonder to me why he'd ever look at Mrs. Collins when he had you to look at. I mean, if I was in his shoes . . ."

Eloise gave a small scornful snort. The evening at the movies had been the same as all the others. Jack had lounged against her, one arm draped along the back of her seat. During the love scenes his breathing had quickened, and he had slipped one hand down over her shoulder. After a minute, as if realizing suddenly what part of her anatomy swelled against his fingers, he had sat up straight and looked around, making such a to-do about getting settled again that he was still squirming when the picture ended and the lights came on. Sighing, Eloise had watched the nestled couples untwining themselves, blinking at this harsh intrusion on their privacy, as they hurried out into the night to take up where they had left off.

"What say we take the short cut?" Jack helped her over a stone wall. A path ran through the fields, past a grove of beech trees. Beyond the trees was her aunt's house.

When they came to the grove Jack said in an off-hand way, "Want to sit down for a while?"

He spread his jacket on the grass and Eloise sat down mopishly. He settled beside her, with his back against a tree.

"You mad at me or something?" he asked after a time.

"Why should I be mad?"

"I don't know. I just thought you acted kind of mad. Whyn't you lean back, then?"

Eloise allowed herself to sink back against him. He hitched forward and put his arms around her, his hands folded across her bosom, his cheek resting against her hair. For a moment she thought he might be working up to something, then dismissed the idea as preposterous.

"Comfortable?" Jack asked.

She nodded, staring at the lights of the village.

"You can lean back more if you want to."

"I'm all right."

"Anything happen today. I mean, you seem kind of, you know. . . ." While he talked, Jack's hands began furtively exploring.

Eloise considered for a moment, then, hoping her news would not make him forget what he was doing, she said, "I got my notice today."

His hands did stop. "You mean they fired you?"

"Well, she was very nice about it. She said they were all sorry, but they couldn't afford to keep help any longer."

"Some excuse!"

"Well, that's what she said. They let Mr. Newby go, too. I'm tired of working there, anyway. They're all so dull. Nothing ever happens there. I can get a job in the five and ten."

"Then we could have lunch together sometimes." Jack resumed his exploring. "I'm glad you're not going to be around that Mr. Richards, anyway. You're not still mad at me for saying that about him chasing you?"

"Well, I don't know where you got the idea I was that kind of a girl. I mean, I've never given you occasion to think I was that kind of a girl, have I?"

"You certainly haven't," he agreed regretfully.

"I mean, some girls are so common," she said, lying back with her hands behind her head.

"Yes." He lay down beside her.

"Letting people take liberties. . . ."

He began to take a few liberties himself.

"I'd be ashamed to look people in the face if I did the things some girls do."

He could only murmur, for his love-making was progressing from one stage to the next.

"Did you ever do this before?" he asked a little later.

"You needn't be insulting!" She clung to him, her eyes shut tight. "Did *you*?" she asked, pushing his head up to see his face.

But his attention was elsewhere and he did not answer. "You haven't even introduced me to your family yet."

"I'll tell Mum to ask you for supper on Sunday," he promised.

"To tell them we're engaged?"

"Engaged?"

"Well, I hope you don't think I'd do this with a person I wasn't engaged to!"

"No, of course not," he said hastily, and covered her mouth with his, to silence her.

The telephone rang once, around ten-thirty. Mrs. Bigelow was halfway downstairs in the dark when Dolly spoke from the hall below. "It was a wrong number, Mother."

"Are you still crying, for heaven's sake?"

"I keep worrying about Homer."

"Oh, pooh!"

"He might lose his head and do something foolish."

"Ha, ha," Mrs. Bigelow said disparagingly, and went back to her room. It was a warm moonless night, bright with stars. George had bought a book on stars and they had spent several evenings lying flat on their backs on garden chairs, studying the constellations. That was before he had proposed. Lately, because of her inability to give him a definite answer, he had lost interest in such pastimes, and the lessons had stopped; but she recognized the Big Dipper, and the kite-shape of Bootes with its bright tail-star. Perversely, she switched on the light to shut out the view of the sky and the Milky Way and the plumed trees outlined against it. Perhaps George had taken someone else to the theater; one of those village widows who were always chasing him. Some of them were younger, prettier, than Mrs. Bigelow. But George had once said that they were a dull lot. And so they are, she told herself. One thing about me, I haven't let myself get in a rut. I've kept up with the times. Kept myself attractive, too. She glanced in the mirror and was chagrined to find that she looked far from attractive, with her hair wind-blown and her make-up fading. At least I'm not dull, she thought defiantly, but she was unable to comfort herself.

When Homer came in half an hour later she went down-stairs.

"I hope you didn't leave the body lying around just anywhere," she said. "I hope you disposed of it properly. The one thing you must remember is that nobody can accuse you of murder unless they find a body. What did you do with it? Did you bury it in the garden?"

"Mother, please," Dolly said.

"Well, he said he was going to kill Claude. I take it for granted he wasn't simply making an idle statement."

"I didn't find them," Homer said.

"Well, tomorrow's another day. You can try again. But if I were you I'd give some thought to the disposal of the body. Don't just leave it lying around. That's where most people make their mistake."

"If you don't mind, Mother, I'd like to have a talk with Dolly," Homer said without looking up. "Alone," he added after a moment, raising his eyes to meet his mother-in-law's sharp glance.

She drew herself up. "I had no idea I was in the way. I wish you had told me earlier."

"I simply want to be alone with Dolly for a few minutes."

"I will go to my room, then. Perhaps you'll be good enough to let me know when I'm allowed to come down again."

"We'll have a nice cup of tea later," Dolly said placatingly.

"Do, by all means. And don't worry about me. I'll be quite content with a drink of water from the bathroom tap."

"I meant all of us. I'll call you when it's ready."

"Don't inconvenience yourself on my account." Mrs. Bigelow went up the stairs with slow and dignified steps. She felt so utterly forsaken and forlorn that she did not even try to overhear what Homer and Dolly were saying.

"I hope I haven't offended her," Homer said, staring at the door where his mother-in-law had disappeared.

"You worry too much about other people's feelings. She was not sparing of yours."

"I can scarcely blame her for getting what fun she can out of my weaknesses. She knows that when I make threats I have no intention of carrying them out." Homer walked around the room, examining the pictures and ornaments with a wistful expression, then sat down. "I'm pretty certain Frank didn't come here tonight to look at the garden," he said.

"Why did he come, then? He couldn't possibly know anything about Claude."

"I'm not so sure. I think he does know something, or suspect something. He kept asking questions."

"About Claude?"

"Yes, he asked how long I'd known Claude, where he'd spent the years since he grew up, and so on. He was rather too off-hand about it, as if he didn't want me to suspect that his interest was anything but casual. And to top everything, he asked to see that old well in the cellar."

"Why?"

"I couldn't figure that one out, myself. He couldn't have known what is in that room. Perhaps he was just being curious. I had told him about the well myself, weeks ago, before Claude came. I told him how finding the old well in the cellar had given me an idea for a book; how I was going to start the story with the discovery of this body in the well, and all the rest of the book was going to deal with unravelling the mystery—whose body it was, and who put it there. I thought Frank might be able to help me with the technical details. I know nothing of how the police go about solving a mystery, you know. Frank thought it was a great idea. He keeps asking me how I'm getting along with the book. I wish I could tell him I'm working on it, but I just can't seem to concentrate these days, with everything so uncertain."

"What did you say, when he asked to see the well?"

"I told him we were putting in a new heating system, and that the furnace room was closed off for the time being. I think he believed me."

"He couldn't know about that room. We can't be sure, ourselves, what Claude is doing with all that machinery he's got down there."

"*I* know. That's what I wanted to tell you. After Frank left I got so worried I decided it was high time I found out what Claude is up to, so I ripped the padlock off the furnace room door. Claude's been doing exactly what we thought he was: printing twenty-dollar bills." Homer took a folded bill from his pocket and handed it to Dolly. "There's a sample."

Dolly spread the bill on her knee. "Claude made this?"

"He's got a pile of them down there a yard high. Or

had. I threw a couple of bundles in the old well, then I thought they should be saved for evidence, so I left the rest."

"Evidence?"

"Yes. I'm going to Frank in the morning and tell him what's been going on. Unless I'm mistaken, he already knows, or suspects. That's why he came here tonight. That's why he asked so many questions. I had already decided, before you came home, to tell him, and what you told me about Grace only strengthened my decision. I just can't *understand* Grace," Homer interrupted himself. "To go running around with a man like Claude. I should think any woman could tell, just by looking at him. . . ."

"Grace is bored. She hasn't enough to occupy her time."

"Then why doesn't she *get* something to occupy it?"

"We'll have to tell her about Claude."

"Only about his counterfeiting," Homer warned. "We're not going to tell anyone, not even Grace, who Claude really is. If someone stumbles on the truth—that he is my cousin—we'll deny it. We'll stick to the story Claude himself made up—that I knew him when he was a boy."

"What if the police find out. What if Claude himself tells them?"

"It's Claude's word against mine. How can he prove that he is my cousin?"

"Fingerprints and things," Dolly said vaguely.

"Well, if he can prove it, we may lose Aunt Harriet's money. That's a chance we'll have to take."

"Lately I've felt that it *was* Aunt Harriet's money, not ours—that it might be snatched from us at any minute."

"I'll see Frank first thing in the morning," Homer said. "Perhaps you could persuade your mother and Grace to spend the day in town with you. You could take the nine-thirty train. Better still, Mr. Newby could drive you in. That would get him out of the way, too. He can take the new car, which will leave Claude without means of transportation—keep him here at home where we want him. We can give Eloise the day off. I'll drive her back to the village when I go to see Frank. We needn't worry about Raymond, he'll sleep until noon. . . . So what we'll do," Homer summed up, "we'll all go off fairly early in the morning—say, by nine-thirty—leaving Claude here by himself. Then I'll bring Frank back, and Frank will make the arrest. He'll certainly have evidence enough, with that pile of counterfeit money in the furnace room."

"Well. . . ." Dolly wrinkled her forehead doubtfully.

"And don't say anything to your mother, or to Grace. The less they know about this, beforehand, the better. Later on, of course, they'll have to know. I suppose it's useless to hope the whole village won't hear about it—about the arrest, I mean."

"Are you sure this is going to work out?"

"You said yourself we can't go on like this."

Dolly gave a long sigh. "I hope nothing goes wrong. . . . If Claude succeeds in proving that he is your aunt Harriet's son, will he get all the money?"

Homer shrugged resignedly. "I could get a job," he said after a time. "Perhaps I could get a better job than the one I had before; one I'd like better, at any rate. I might even find something in the village. The people here like me, I think. . . . Having this money, even for so short a time, has done something for me. It's given me confidence. I used to feel like apologizing all the time—not only to you, but to everyone else as well—because I was not a success. I used to wonder what people thought of me. Now it doesn't seem to matter."

"We were happy for a little while," Dolly said, as if this explained everything. "When people say, 'Money isn't important', and 'Money won't buy happiness,' as if there were some virtue in being poor, I wonder what they mean. Phrases invented to console the poor," she added in a contemptuous voice.

"We may soon have to use those phrases to console ourselves."

"Yes."

"You mustn't cry," Homer said, patting her shoulder.

"I only want to go on being happy."

"We must hope for the best," Homer said, but his expression was not hopeful.

Chapter Nine

WAKING to brilliant sunshine the next morning, Mrs. Bigelow felt old and tired. "And no wonder," she said, peering at herself in the mirror, believing that she had not closed her eyes all night. She had been wakened once, shortly after midnight, by Claude coming in. Now she could hear him snoring in his room across the hall.

She went downstairs. Breakfast had been laid on the terrace. "Am I late?" she asked in a cross voice, seeing Dolly and Homer had already eaten.

"It's almost nine."

"You might have called me," Mrs. Bigelow grumbled, poking suspiciously at a pile of cold toast.

"Eloise is making fresh toast," Dolly said, "and scrambled eggs. She'll be along with them in a minute. I've telephoned Grace and persuaded her to spend the day with us in town. Mr. Newby's driving us in. We're leaving in half an hour."

"I can't go. I have other business to attend to."

"What other business?" Homer laid aside the newspaper he was pretending to read.

"Various things," Mrs. Bigelow said cryptically. She had made up her face too carefully. Her rosy cheeks emphasized the circles under her eyes. Immediately after breakfast she meant to telephone George. She would spend the entire day, if necessary, explaining about last night.

"But I've planned this trip especially so that we can talk to Grace," Dolly said. "You said yourself, last night . . ." She stopped as Eloise, wearing a woolgathering smile, came from the kitchen carrying Mrs. Bigelow's breakfast on a tray.

"What have *you* been up to?" Mrs. Bigelow demanded, as Eloise placed the tray before her.

"Nothing." Eloise cast her eyes down, all innocence.

"You're looking mighty pleased with yourself. Like the cat that swallowed the canary. Have you been carrying on with that young man of yours?"

Eloise looked shocked.

"You make him behave himself," Mrs. Bigelow admonished. "Don't let him start any nonsense." She watched Eloise's rounded figure disappear. Her advice had been given automatically, with no expectation that it would be followed. "It's a good thing someone can smile around here," she remarked.

"Mother, about today. . . ."

"Grace's problems will have to wait. I have problems of my own today."

"But I'd *counted* on you."

"It's not a matter of life or death, after all. I don't see why you both look so fidgety."

"I wish you'd reconsider, Mother."

"I have my own life to live."

"There is a special reason why Dolly wants you to go with her," Homer began.

"After the sacrifices I've made," his mother-in-law continued, hearing only her own voice, beginning to enjoy herself, "is it unnatural for me to think of myself for a change—of my own happiness? No one ever considers that *I* have feelings, too."

"What is wrong, Mother?"

"You wouldn't understand."

"Perhaps I could help."

"I only want to be left alone. Is that too much to ask?" Mrs. Bigelow pressed one hand to her forehead in a tragic gesture and went to telephone George.

"You've missed Dad again," Lola said. Her voice was openly amused now. "He's just left for the village. I don't believe he'll be back for some time."

"Did you give him my message?"

"He was rather busy," Lola answered evasively.

Mrs. Bigelow slammed down the receiver.

"What is it, Mother?" Dolly asked, coming down the stairs with her hat and gloves on.

"Nothing. I'm going to the village."

"Homer is going to the village. He'll drive you. Homer!" Dolly called. "Mother is going to the village with you."

"Oh, good! I'll be ready in five minutes." Homer came in from the terrace, looking so relieved that Mrs. Bigelow wondered.

"I didn't realize you were that anxious for my company," she said, and went upstairs to fetch her handbag. On the landing she met Claude coming down. He was wearing his striped silk bathrobe.

"*Hel*-lo, Auntie!" He lifted her by the elbows and swung her around, then as she hunched herself away disdainfully, pretended to be hurt. "Oh, Auntie, you're not mad at me?"

"I'll deal with you later," she said grimly.

"You do that, Auntie. We'll have a cozy chat."

He was not so cheerful when she came downstairs

again. The coffee was cold, and Eloise was telling him that, since she had been given the day off, she had no time to prepare another breakfast.

"Who is going to cook it, then?" he asked, wrinkling his forehead, trying to look pathetic.

For a change, Eloise was not taken in by his winning ways. "I couldn't say, I'm sure," she said.

He glanced through the window and his face darkened. "Who is using my car?" he asked sharply.

"*Your* car?" Mrs. Bigelow gave him a good stare. "It just so happens that Mr. Newby is driving that car to the city this morning."

"We'll see about that," Claude said, but before he reached the door Mr. Newby, with Grace and Dolly in the back seat, had driven away. Homer stood in the drive-way seeing them off. He waved, then gathered up some garden tools that Mr. Newby had been using and carried them to the cellar. Claude followed him. Sharp words ensued.

"Are they quarrelling?" Eloise was all ears.

"Of course not." Mrs. Bigelow was trying to listen without appearing to do so.

"It certainly sounds like it," Eloise insisted.

"So you've been given the day off."

"Yes. Mrs. Flynn said, since you're all going to be away today, I might as well have a holiday, too."

"Well, it's a nice day for a holiday." Mrs. Bigelow was trying to pretend that nothing unusual was going on, though it was quite evident, now, that Homer and Claude were having a heated argument. "We'll wait in the car," she said, and led Eloise outside.

Eloise, though she had not caught the drift of the argument in the cellar, and now was entirely beyond earshot, sat in the car and planned how she would describe the battle to her friends. "Shouting and swearing at one another," she would say. "Oh, it was terrible."

When Homer came out, alone, she was disappointed to note that he showed no signs of having been in a struggle. She had hoped to see, at the very least, a black eye. He merely looked grim.

"Ready?" He climbed behind the wheel of his black sedan and drove in silence to the village.

"All right if I drop you both off here?" he asked, stopping in front of the five and ten. "I'll pick you up at the post office in, say, an hour," he told his mother-in-law. "If I'm late, wait for me." He drove away.

Mrs. Bigelow had already caught sight of George's convertible parked some distance up the street. As she walked toward it, she rehearsed her apologies. She would not say that she had forgotten about last night—she could scarcely expect him to forgive her for that—but she would tell him the truth up to a point. "What mother wouldn't be upset?" she would say, after she had dramatized her dash to the village to save Grace from her folly. "Could any mother think of herself at such a time?" George would understand. He would say, "I'd have done the same thing myself." He would not find it necessary to remind her that Grace was forty years old, and presumably mature enough to extricate herself from her own follies.

The door of the supermarket swung open and George came out, carrying a large bag of groceries. Then he turned and, burdened as he was, offered his arm to the woman at his side. Mrs. Bigelow backed into a shop doorway, then into the shop itself, as they walked toward her. The woman smiled up at George. The brim of her wide hat scraped his chin as they jogged along.

She was young, not more than sixty, with a plump pretty face. A very ordinary type, Mrs. Bigelow decided,

taking in every detail from her vantage point behind a
window display of parchment lampshades. Her hat was
pale blue straw trimmed with forget-me-nots and a black
velvet ribbon tied in a bow at the back. Her dress would
have suited a girl of seventeen. It was pale blue also, a
sheer material that gave glimpses of a lace-trimmed slip
and the rolls of flesh above it. She wore high-heeled
white sandals. Her ankles were slim. George would
appreciate that. He liked nice legs.

"May I help you, madam?" A clerk came up behind
Mrs. Bigelow so quietly that she jumped.

"Help me?" She looked at him with a vague puzzled
expression. "Oh, yes. . . ." She picked up the first article
that came to hand, a pottery planter of extreme ugliness,
shaped like a fat spotted dog. "How much is this?"

"That one is ninety-eight cents." He waited a minute,
then said, "We have some very nice ones at two dollars. . . . And these copper ones at three-fifty."

Mrs. Bigelow threw a glance out the window and saw
that George was helping his companion into his car. He
then walked around and sat in the driver's seat, but did
not immediately drive away. Instead, he leaned on the
steering wheel, listening with what appeared to be great
interest, while his companion talked.

"Were you looking for something as a gift?" the clerk
inquired.

"Yes. . . . Yes, a gift."

"These tole trays are popular. Handy for serving
drinks."

Mrs. Bigelow turned the tray over and looked at the
bottom, then laid it aside.

"Or how about one of these figurines? Makes a lovely
ornament."

George must have said something extremely funny,

for the woman with him slapped his arm and burst into a shrill giggle. When she had stopped laughing he backed out of the parking space and drove away.

"Or this set of long-handled forks," the clerk suggested. "Has your friend got a barbeque?"

"I'll take the figurine," Mrs. Bigelow said.

"Shall I gift-wrap it?"

"No, a bag will do."

"That will be five dollars, then. I'm sure your friend will be pleased."

"What?"

"I said I'm sure your friend will like the figurine."

"Oh . . . yes."

"That will be five dollars."

Mrs. Bigelow had no idea why she had bought the figurine, unless it was because, for the moment, she did not know what else to do. Out on the street, she stood looking up and down in an undecided way, then walked to the station and from there took a taxi home to Dove Cottage.

She let herself in the front door and went to the kitchen, where she made a cup of instant coffee and, in an excess of despondency, smoked one of Claude's cigarettes. I might as well go to hell with myself, she thought. What have I got to live for? Dragging in great puffs of smoke, she was seized with a fit of coughing, and hoped it was tubercular. What a fool I was to think he cared! she mourned. The pangs of jealousy—or perhaps it was the cigarette—made her dizzy, and she put one hand to her brow in an unconsciously theatrical gesture. She was doomed to live in someone else's house for the rest of her days, to accept the charity of her daughter's husband.

Her own unselfishness had brought her to this. She ought to have said yes when George first asked her to marry him, snatched at the chance without a thought for anyone else. "I have sacrificed myself for them," she said aloud, meaning Homer and Dolly.

The sound of her own voice startled her. The house was too quiet. Claude should be somewhere about, in his room, or carrying on his mysterious experiments in the cellar. She went to the head of the cellar stairs to listen. There was no sound from the furnace room. Perhaps he had gone out. She would just look and see if by any chance he had left the door of the furnace room unlocked.

The door was ajar, she saw, as she went down the steps. Cautiously she pushed it open and went inside, groping in the half-dark for a light. When her eyes became accustomed to the gloom she found one and turned it on.

There was no need to look twice at the printing press on the workbench in the center of the room. Its function was clearly advertised by the pile of crisp currency which had been tossed upon the bench with apparent carelessness. So Homer was right, she thought, Claude *has* been making money down here. A number of bills—they appeared to be all twenties—had fallen to the floor. She picked one up and examined it, feeling as excited as if she had stumbled upon a genuine treasure. It certainly looked like the real thing. It might not fool a bank clerk, but any shopkeeper would accept it without question. A wild idea flashed through her mind. Why not—since she was loveless and rejected—take a pile of these bills and have one last fling? Go on a trip to Paris, Rome, Timbuctoo, all the places she had never been, and ease her broken heart with riotous living. By the time the police caught up with her the money would be all spent. They might put her in jail, but what difference would that make? Her life was as good as over.

Behind her, the cold furnace creaked, and she whirled around. Tubs of last winter's ashes were lined up along the wall. Homer, with his usual lack of system, had never gotten around to removing them.

She noted also that the cover was off the old well. How stupid of Claude to work beside that gaping hole, she thought. What if he stepped into it? It would be the solution to everything, she answered herself. No, not everything. It would not bring George back.

On the alert for sounds which would indicate that Claude was returning from wherever he was, she began hurriedly to collect the money. Perhaps she would go to the South Seas instead of Paris, and when she had spent all the money she could throw herself into a volcano. She had seen that done in movies. Of course there was always the chance that she might meet someone to take George's place—some lonely millionaire, for instance.

A small bundle of bills was lying, wavering, at the very edge of the open well. She stooped to pick it up, but it went over the rim out of sight. She knelt and peered into the depths. Dark as pitch. An extension cord, with a light bulb enclosed in wire mesh, was looped over a nail at one end of the bench. Curiosity prompted her to turn this on and lower it into the well. Claude, wearing his striped silk bathrobe, was lying at the bottom. He was dead. He could not be anything but dead, in that position.

She pulled up the cord and looped it over the nail as she had found it. Then she ran up the two flights of stairs to her own room. She began to shake, and clutched at the bedpost for support.

I never thought Homer would do it, was all she could

think. I never thought for one minute he'd actually *do* it! Last night when he had threatened to kill Claude she had been fool enough to laugh at Dolly for taking his threat seriously. The laugh was on her now. Homer had meant what he said. She recalled how he had been so anxious to get everybody out of the house that morning, sending Mr. Newby off to town with Dolly and Grace, giving Eloise the day off. He had wanted the house to himself. But why had he done it *before* he got everybody out of the way? He must have done it while she and Eloise were waiting in the car. He had come stalking up the cellar steps, after his quarrel with Claude, looking so grim and determined. He had not said one word on the way to the village, but had stared straight ahead as if hypnotized.

What desperation must have driven him to such a deed! she thought, feeling an unaccustomed wave of admiration and pity for Homer. To *plan* such a deed; for there could be no doubt that the act was premeditated, done with malice aforethought. He must have lain awake all night planning how he would execute his crime. Or had the crime been committed on the spur of the moment? Had the opportunity presented itself so suddenly that Homer had acted without thinking; could that explain why he had panicked before the job was finished and left Claude there to advertise his presence? . . . which he would surely do, and very soon, in the heat of summer.

It was just like Homer to bungle the job. He had committed the perfect crime, then lost his nerve in the middle of it and rushed off, probably to throw himself into the nearest river.

She sank down on the bed and covered her eyes, then suddenly sat up again. Homer might salve his own conscience by jumping into the river, but a lot of good that would do the rest of them. He's left us holding the bag, she thought resentfully. Left us to face the police, the reporters, to answer questions—even, perhaps, bear the punishment for his crime. *I* might be accused of killing Claude. She stood up and paced the room, beating her hands together, unable to bear the picture which leaped to her mind: herself behind prison bars, growing old, dying, in a cold cell; perhaps even suffering a worse death, a quicker one.

Even if Homer were blamed for Claude's death, she reasoned, everyone at Dove Cottage would suffer. Poor Dolly would be disgraced forever, branded the wife of a murderer. "Someone must finish the job, for Dolly's sake," Mrs. Bigelow said aloud.

She scuttled into Claude's room, gathered up an armful of clothes, and carried them to the cellar, where she dropped them into the well. She made three more trips. Every stitch of clothing, every belonging of Claude's, she tossed into the well on top of him. Then she dragged four tubs of ashes across the floor and dumped them in, too. Panting, she ran upstairs again, washed her face and changed her dress and shoes. She threw the dress she had been wearing, which was stained with ashes, into the back of her closet.

She had not quite finished cleaning up when she heard a car in the yard. Looking out, she saw Homer drive up. Behind him, in his own car, was Frank Gates. Homer had not thrown himself into the river then, he had done something ever more foolish: he had gone to the police. "So you've given yourself up, you damned fool," Mrs. Bigelow said silently. "I suppose it's never occurred to you that *we* will be the ones to suffer." She watched Frank and Homer as they walked across the yard. They were talking seriously, but apparently in a friendly way. Homer was not handcuffed. He led Frank in through the back door and down into the cellar.

I must do what I can to save him, Mrs. Bigelow thought. I'll lie. I'll tell Frank that Claude attacked first, that Homer struck him in self-defense. But how explain why Claude had been thrown into the well? I'll think of something, she told herself as she went downstairs. She stood outside the furnace room door, spying on them, determined to learn how much Frank knew before she presented her story.

Frank had scooped up a handful of bills and was examining them under the light. "They're the same ones, all right," he said. "See this little mark in the lower corner? That's the giveaway. Same plates as he used in Chicago. It'll be a feather in our caps, I can tell you, coming up with this fellow. The Chicago police were pretty red-faced when he gave them the slip."

They put their heads together under the light. Their shadows loomed on the wall behind them.

"Imagine him trying to palm these off right under our noses," Frank said. "I suppose he thought we were just a bunch of hick cops."

"I don't believe he realized that he *had* spent one in the village until after he'd done it," Homer said. "According to what he said this morning, these phony bills were so good they even fooled him. He had the nerve to joke about it."

"He'll soon change his tune," Frank remarked. His eyes roved around the room. "Say, is that the old well?"

Homer glanced over his shoulder and nodded. "That's it."

Mrs. Bigelow marvelled at his composure. She expected him to be cowed, apologetic, apprehensive, plain

scared, anything but what he was. Even when Frank
sauntered over to the well and bent to look into it,
Homer's expression did not change. He leaned against the
workbench, idly sorting over some tools he had found
there, weighing them in his hand, testing the feel of
them.

"Kind of dangerous, leaving this hole wide open like
this, isn't it?" Frank straightened up. "First thing you
know, somebody's going to fall in."

"I opened it up last night." Homer laid aside the tools
he was playing with and went to stand beside Frank.
Both gazed into the well. "When I found this stuff last
night," he waved toward the workbench, "my first idea
was to throw everything down the well—get rid of it.
Then I realized how foolish that would be."

"Good thing you didn't," Frank said. "We'd have had
to dig it all up again, as evidence. Give me a hand with
this thing, Homer. I'm not going to have it on my
conscience if anybody falls in." He bent to lift the heavy
cover, then straightened. "Say, isn't it kind of funny Mr.
Richards hasn't come down to see what we're doing
down here?"

"I was thinking the same thing. I don't even hear him
moving around upstairs." Homer lifted one corner of the
well cover, Frank the other, and they fitted it into place
over the opening. "Maybe he fell in here," Homer
suggested in a joking voice. "Think we ought to look?"

Mrs. Bigelow held her breath, but Frank grinned and
said, "If he's in there, he can stay." He flexed the muscles
of his hands. "That thing weighs a ton."

"He's probably in his room. I'll go find him." Homer
turned and saw his mother-in-law. "I thought you were
in the village. How did you get home?"

"I took a taxi."

"Oh, I see. Well, I'll explain about all this later. Nothing to be alarmed about. Right now I've got to find Claude."

So that was his story. He was going to pretend he didn't know where Claude was. He had gone to Frank, not to confess that he had disposed of Claude by throwing him into the well, but simply to report that he had discovered a machine for making money in his cellar. It didn't quite make sense, but then Homer had never been what you might call nimble-witted. Or perhaps he was being very crafty indeed. Leaving the cover off the well was certainly an ingenious manouver. It lessened the temptation to look inside. And allowing Frank to replace the cover himself was downright clever. A bit too clever, perhaps. Homer was tempting Providence with his daring. Mrs. Bigelow stood aside to let him pass. "Let's go up," he said. "Claude must be somewhere in the house."

In the kitchen, while Homer was upstairs, Frank lit a cigarette and smiled at Mrs. Bigelow. "I guess you're wondering what this is all about?"

"Yes, I am." She might as well hear his version.

"Well, in the first place, it seems that this fellow who's been palming himself off as Homer's old friend Mr. Richards, isn't Mr. Richards at all. His name's Jones, Jesse Jones—at least that's what he's been calling himself. Probably isn't his real name. He was serving a prison term in Chicago; for passing counterfeit money, among other things. Oh, he's quite a character, this fellow. A real smart guy. Always cooking up fraudulent schemes. He's swindled I don't know how many people out of their life's savings. Homer tells me he borrowed quite a sum of money from *him*—I don't wonder you look thunderstruck," he interrupted, eyeing Mrs. Bigelow with concern, "discovering that the man you thought was an old friend of Homer's is an escaped convict. Maybe you'd better sit down."

Mrs. Bigelow allowed him to help her to a chair.

"What gets me is him picking on a nice fellow like Homer, palming himself off as an old friend Homer hadn't seen for thirty years. You know Homer's the type that thinks everybody's as honest as himself. Naturally he was taken in. The only thing I'm wondering is how this fellow knew Homer hadn't seen the real Claude Richards for thirty years."

"Who told you all this?" Mrs. Bigelow asked. If Frank got to wondering too much, he might discover there were other points that could not be explained.

"Well, we get these circulars from various cities, descriptions of wanted criminals. We got a bunch—oh, about a week after this fellow came to visit Homer. One circular gave a description of this Jesse Jones, wanted in Chicago. His picture was on it. I said to one of the boys, kind of joking, 'This fellow's a dead ringer for that famous author that's staying at the Flynn's place.' I never thought any more about it until this counterfeit money turned up in the village. I sent one of the bills— the first one that turned up, over a week ago—down to Washington, and they wired back that it was undoubtedly the work of this fellow Jones. I started to put two and two together, but I didn't like to say anything to Homer. A nice fellow like that, I didn't see how he could be mixed up with any underworld characters. So I drove over to Greenwood this morning to see if the boys there had picked up any clues, and when I got back Homer was waiting in my office to tell me he'd caught his house guest making money in the cellar, and what should he do about it."

Frank leaned against the counter and pushed up his cap to scratch his head. "There's a couple of points we haven't ironed out yet," he went on, "but we've caught the criminal—with the goods, too. We'll sweat the details out of him later."

I wouldn't count on that, Mrs. Bigelow thought.

Homer came downstairs. "How long have you been here, Mother?"

"Forty-five minutes, perhaps, or an hour. Why?"

"It's the funniest thing . . . !" Homer rubbed his forehead in a puzzled way. He beckoned to Frank. "Come upstairs a minute. I want to show you something."

The two men went upstairs and Mrs. Bigelow followed. "Every stitch of clothing gone!" Homer pointed dramatically to the empty closet in Claude's room. "Bureau drawers empty. All his belongings gone. What do you make of that?"

"You don't mean to say he's got away?" Frank's face reddened with disappointment.

"I don't see how he could have got away. I wasn't gone more than an hour and a half, and I made sure he was left here without means of transportation. Mr. Newby took the new car into town, and I was driving our old car, so if Claude did get away, how did he do it?"

"He might have called a taxi."

"He wouldn't get far in a taxi. He'd miss the last morning train, and there isn't another one until mid-afternoon."

Homer's portrayal of bewildered innocence rivalled the performance of a great actor, Mrs. Bigelow thought. She supposed that desperation had brought out qualities in him that he never knew he possessed. She was surprised to find herself admiring him, wanting to help him for his own sake, not just because by protecting him she would be saving Dolly too. As they filed downstairs to the kitchen, she hastily decided on the story she would tell.

Frank took out a notebook, glanced at the clock, and made a note. "You say you returned from the village an hour ago, Mrs. Bigelow? That would be nine-forty-five. You saw no sign of Claude?"

"I didn't say that. As a matter of fact, I did see him. If I had known what this was all about, if you had taken me into your confidence, Homer, I would have told you sooner. But you didn't see fit to tell me. I was kept completely in the dark." Mrs. Bigelow was rather admiring her own performance. She assumed an expression of bewildered indignation that put Homer's acting to shame.

"He was here when you returned from the village?" Frank asked.

"Yes."

"Did you see him leave?"

"Well, yes, I suppose I did." She had always noticed, in television plays, that when those questioned were innocent parties, telling the truth, their answers were stumbling and halting. They got mixed up, could not remember details. The guilty ones always answered glibly. She decided that she must be convincingly hesitant and muddle-headed.

"You *suppose* you did? Don't you know?"

"Let me see, now." She placed the tips of her fingers against her forehead and closed her eyes. "I came home from the village about—well, I'm not sure what time it was. Less than an hour ago. I took the village taxi. The driver could tell you. I had bought a figurine in the village, a little china shepherdess. . . ."

"So when you got here, Claude was in the house? Did you speak to him?"

"I didn't actually see him then. I just assumed he was somewhere in the house. I went up to my room. Then I saw a car drive into the yard."

"What kind of a car?"

"A blue one. Or perhaps it was gray."

"A late model?"

"I couldn't be sure. I think it had a radio aerial—you know, one of those aluminum rods—with a squirrel tail. Or a coon tail. . . ." In her mind's eye she now saw the car, a gray coupe about ten years old, with battered fenders and tarnished chrome. "It was a gray car," she said, opening her eyes. "The man driving it was wearing a white undershirt. His arms looked pale and pimply. Quite a thin man, dark. . . ."

"Did he get out?"

"I'm not sure. I . . ." She lowered her eyes and tried to blush. "I had to go to the bathroom. If you had only *told* me!" she cried, glaring at Homer. "If I had been given some *inkling* of what was going on, I might have been more observant. But I didn't know. You saw fit to keep me in the dark."

"I can understand Homer not wanting to frighten you," Frank said placatingly. "Did you catch a glimpse of Claude at all?"

"The next time I looked out, Claude was getting into this gray car. Did I tell you it had a coon tail on the aerial? Then it drove away."

"Which direction?"

"North, I *think*." She looked doubtful.

"Did Claude have any bags with him?"

"I didn't see any. He could have put them in the car when I was in the—when I wasn't looking."

Frank turned a page of his notebook and kept on scribbling. "Now, I want you to think hard, Mrs.

Bigelow, and tell me if you remember anything else. Any little thing."

She thought hard, and shook her head.

"Well, I'll phone this to the boys." Frank went to the telephone in the hall. Alone with Homer, Mrs. Bigelow found that she could not meet his eyes. She busied herself at the sink, washing out some dirty cups.

"I've sent the boys out after him," Frank reported, coming in from the hall. "Damn it, I hope he hasn't slipped through our fingers." He sat down, stared moodily at his notebook, then snapped it shut and thrust it into his breast pocket.

"It's my fault if he has escaped," Homer said. "I should have come to you last night when I discovered the set-up in the cellar."

"It would have helped," Frank admitted. "Why didn't you?"

"Well, I was so surprised, I guess I didn't think. In the first place, I could hardly believe that Claude could be mixed up in anything like that; then I got to thinking what people would say when they heard about it."

"Sure, I can understand you being pretty upset, a thing like this happening in your home. I don't see how we're going to keep it quiet, though. It's bound to get in all the newspapers. I sure wish you'd come to me last night."

"Yes, I should have."

"Well, if he has got away, it's partly my fault, I guess," Frank said generously. "If I'd been in my office this morning instead of chasing clues over in Greenwood . . . How long did you have to wait?"

"Almost an hour, I guess. Nobody seemed to know where you were."

Frank looked sheepish. "Matter of fact, I stopped off for a beer," he said. "But don't tell anyone that. I'll have to think up a good excuse if those city police come snooping. They make me sick, always barging in when something big happens. I might just throw them off the scent by saying Claude got a *two*-hour start on us. But don't you worry," he added. "We'll pick him up. And I'd say you handled your end of it pretty well, Homer, considering. I'll put that in my report."

"You'll never catch Claude," Mrs. Bigelow stated positively.

"I wouldn't be too sure of that." Frank slapped his pockets and adjusted his cap, which he had not taken off. "I'd better be off—see how the boys are making out. I'll keep in touch with you."

Homer saw him to the door.

"I'll send the boys over to pick up that stuff in the cellar," Frank said.

"Right you are," Homer answered. "And let me know the minute you get a report on the fugitive."

"I'll do that. See you later, Homer."

Chapter Ten

WELL, that's that!" Homer said in a tone of relief as he closed the door. "Do you feel like a cup of coffee, Mother?" While she put the coffee on, he cut a slice of bread and spread it with butter and marmalade. "I didn't eat much breakfast," he explained.

"Would you like a boiled egg as well?"

"This will do. I don't want to spoil my lunch." He finished the bread and cut off another slice.

She watched him, appalled by his coolness. How *could* he sit there stuffing himself, after what he had done?

"I think everything went off very well, don't you?" he asked, digging a great scoop of marmalade out of the jar and licking the spoon. "I can't tell you what a relief it was to hear you say that Claude had got away. It will simplify everything. If he's got an hour's start on the police, I don't think there's much chance of them catching him, do you?" He looked up with what she took to be deceitful candor.

"I'd be very much surprised if they do," she said.

"Frank didn't suspect a thing, did you notice? I believe we're safe. If they did catch up with Claude, and he told them who he really is, we might find ourselves in hot water, but," he held out his cup to be filled, "I've got a feeling Mr. Claude Richards isn't going to bother us for a while. What do you think?" he asked with bare-faced guile.

"I'm quite sure of it," Mrs. Bigelow agreed. Her hand was not steady as she poured the coffee, for now she was beginning to be frightened. If Homer could be so casual about the terrible thing he had done, might he not be capable of other crimes? She had read stories about people suddenly changing, newspaper accounts of timid clerks going berserk with hatchets, staid clergymen chopping up choirgirls, devoted wives all of a sudden longing to become widows and achieving this state through the use of arsenic in ham sandwiches. Multiple personality, she thought, drawing on her limited knowledge of abnormal psychology. She imagined that Homer's general appearance had altered, but when she tried to pinpoint the changes she could not. He simply looked tired and a little hollow-eyed, like a person who, waking from a nightmare, is relieved to find that it is only a nightmare after all.

She went up to her room, pulled down the shades and lay in darkened silence, trying not to dwell on the morning's happenings. Dozing, she dreamed that Claude came up out of the cellar, covered with ashes, and stood accusingly before her. This dream frightened her into wakefulness. In an effort to keep busy she set up her painting equipment and worked for a time on her latest picture. This had been, in the beginning, a self-portrait. Unable to capture a likeness, she had done the next best thing and turned it into a modern design of planes and cubes which she intended to call, simply, "Woman." Yesterday she had considered this painting a masterpiece, but today she fancied that the features had taken on the appearance of a death mask. She turned it to the wall and sat beside the window, staring out. For a time she was diverted by the arrival of Frank Gates and his assistant, who made a commotion removing Claude's machinery from the cellar. A little later, wandering downstairs, she heard Homer in the cellar. She did not want to know what he was doing, but could not help going down to see. He was emptying the last of the ashes into the well.

"That's a job I've been meaning to do since April," he said, dusting off his hands. "The next thing I'm going to do is call up the furnace people and have them install a decent heating unit down here. I might as well do that right now." He went off to telephone.

Finding herself alone in the cellar, Mrs. Bigelow threw a terrified glance behind her and scuttled up the stairs.

"It's away past lunch time," Homer said when he had completed his telephone call. "I cut off a bit of that cold ham for myself. Don't you want anything?"

Mrs. Bigelow shook her head. "I'm not hungry."

"You're feeling all right, though?" He looked at her with some concern.

"No, I don't feel all right." She was near to tears. "I feel awful. All this happening and you being so nonchalant about it. . . . I just don't know what to think."

"I should have warned you. I forgot that you hadn't been told that things might come to a head this morning. Dolly and I decided last night, you see."

"Dolly? Does she know about this?"

"Why, yes. We planned the whole thing last night. That's why she took Grace and Mr. Newby into town this morning, to get them out of the way. That's why we were so anxious for you to go, too. We thought it would be better if I did the job by myself. You see, I discovered last night what Claude was doing in the cellar, so I talked it over with Dolly and we decided it was high time we put an end to the whole business, no matter what the consequences. . . . That's probably Dolly now," he added, as the telephone rang.

Mrs. Bigelow started up the stairs, fearful of what she might hear. Homer's voice pursued her. "Well, it's over, Dolly. We got rid of him. You come on home and I'll tell you all about it."

Mrs. Bigelow put her hands over her ears and ran up to her room. Her head was splitting. She took three aspirins and lay down, this time with a wet towel over her eyes. Think of everyday things, she told herself. Think of rain, of birds, of walking in the park. The pounding in her head soon stopped and she enjoyed a period of convalescence during which her mind simply drifted, avoiding what she did not wish to remember. When her husband died, and she had suffered the shock of learning that he had left her penniless, she had spent a whole week in just such a state of suspended feeling, convinced that when she stirred herself to investigate she would find that it had all been a mistake, that she had in reality been left a comfortable income with which to enjoy her widowhood. That week had in a way been one of the happy times of her life, until well-meaning friends broke the spell with reminders that creditors were hammering at the door.

This afternoon, escaping into dreams again, she was enjoying a tour of the French countryside—the Beaujolais, about which she had recently read—with George, when reality in the shape of Dolly again intruded. She heard the car in the yard, and a short time later Dolly called up the stairs.

Mrs. Bigelow rose, gave her curls a push, and went downstairs. "What is it, Dolly?" she asked in a vexed voice. "I was having a little nap."

"Homer says you saw Claude leaving. I want you to tell me about it."

"Homer knows as much about it as I do."

"We haven't said anything to Grace yet," Dolly went on. "I thought we should get together first and decide how much we're going to tell her—how much we're going to tell other people, too."

"Of course there's still a chance that Claude will be caught," Homer said, "and in that case we may have to change our story to suit the circumstances. It will depend on what he says, though I certainly intend to deny it if he claims any relationship. . . ." He paused to consider various possibilities. "But your mother and I agree that, with an hour's start on the police, Claude's got a very good chance of escaping capture." He spoke with a little too much confidence; as if he were trying to make his words sound convincing, his mother-in-law thought.

"It shows that he was only bluffing," Dolly said. "Running off like that, I mean. It shows he'd rather lose Aunt Harriet's inheritance than allow the police to catch him. I wonder where he is now?" she mused. Her eyes were transparent, entirely innocent.

So Dolly knows nothing of what really happened, her mother thought. She hasn't the faintest idea that Claude is at the bottom of that old well in the furnace room, not out fleeing along the highways.

She turned to look at Homer. He was staring at a jar of delphiniums on the table, chewing a fingernail, wearing a look that was relieved and apprehensive at the same time, one expression not quite cancelling the other. When a shower of blue petals fell suddenly, he started, then tried to pretend that the involuntary movement had merely been a preliminary to shifting his position. Even

179

this small deception was badly executed. All his actions and expressions were as artless as a child's.

Mrs. Bigelow felt a wave of doubt. As Homer repeated for Dolly's benefit his part in the morning's activities, she interrupted him at intervals with sly questions designed to trip him into revealing—to her, not to Dolly—that he knew more than he pretended to know. Not once did he deviate from his original story. A little later he repeated the whole thing to Grace and Raymond.

"Lola telephoned me," Grace said. She was out of breath from hurrying. "I hadn't been in the house five minutes when the phone rang. Lola had apparently been trying to get me all afternoon, but Raymond was sleeping in the garden and didn't hear the bell. She told me some fantastic story about Claude. She had heard it in the village, she said." Grace was trying to appear less upset than she really was. Raymond watched her. "She said Claude has disappeared, and that the police are looking for him."

"Yes, it's true." Homer repeated his story.

"I don't believe it," Grace said.

"Why?" Raymond stared hard at her. "Why don't you believe it?"

She flushed. "It sounds fantastic, that's all."

"I don't know why you're so upset," Raymond said, still watching her. "You told me yourself that you didn't particularly like Claude."

"I'm not upset!"

"I'm very glad to hear it," Raymond said. "For my part, I'm not at all surprised to learn that Claude has turned out to be somebody else, and a criminal to boot. I always thought there was something sneaky about him. But I wonder what the village people would make of it if they knew how you are carrying on."

"I'm not carrying on, for heaven's sake!"

"Then pull yourself together," Raymond said shortly. "Don't act as if the world had come to an end." He turned to Homer and asked some questions, later was taken to the cellar to view the scene of Claude's illicit operations. Afterwards, Homer telephoned Frank Gates to ask if Claude had been found.

"Not a sign of him," he reported as he replaced the receiver. "Frank says they've got every road in the country blocked off, but they're beginning to think Claude's made a clean getaway."

When he went out to the kitchen to prepare a tray of soft drinks, remarking that after what they'd all been through they needed a pick-up, Mrs. Bigelow cornered him. "Did you really expect they'd catch Claude?" she asked.

"Well, I hoped they wouldn't. You must admit that things will be much easier for us if they don't. It will prove, as Dolly mentioned, that he would rather forfeit Aunt Harriet's inheritance than give himself up."

"You knew they wouldn't catch him."

"How could I *know*?" He looked at her with such simple perplexity that her heart sank like a lead weight. He's acting, she kept on telling herself. There's no need to act with *me*, she went on in silent indignation. Pretending you don't know Claude is at the bottom of that old well. If you didn't put him there, who did? She wanted to say this aloud but could not, because by now she was not at all certain that Homer shared with her the secret of the well.

By dinner time she was sure that Homer was entirely innocent. She tried to imagine what must have happened. The only thing she could think of was that Claude had fallen down the well by himself. She remembered the half-darkness of the furnace room, how she had hesitated at the door, trying to accustom her eyes to the dimness before she ventured inside. Claude, knowing his way around, had not hesitated, had not even bothered to turn on the light. And he had stepped into the well without seeing it. That was the way it must have happened.

Which meant that she, Vera Bigelow, was the only person in the world who knew he was there. She picked at her food without appetite. How could she spend the night in this house, which would be forever haunted now? She must tell Dolly and Homer. The whole thing was Homer's fault, after all, for allowing Claude to stay at Dove Cottage in the first place.

She did not want to tell Dolly and Homer, or anyone else. She longed for nothing so much as to forget the whole thing, and for a time hoped that the shock of the morning's discovery would affect her mind, wipe the whole thing from her memory. She waited for this to happen all through the first course of the meal, which was cold ham again, not one of her favorite dishes. She then tried to invent reasons why she should keep her secret to herself. There was no earthly use in hoping that Dolly and Homer would behave sensibly; that is, leave Claude where he was and say nothing. Not them. They would have the shovels out before she could say Peter Piper. That was the trouble with conscientious people. They never stopped to think. And when they had gone to all the bother of digging Claude out, making explanations—which would not sound at all plausible to the police—and of burying him somewhere else—at great expense—think of the gossip in the village! No, it would be better for all concerned to let well enough alone, Mrs. Bigelow decided. Of course it will, she assured herself. Why should I upset everybody?

But her conscience was dissatisfied with these reasons why she should not speak up. It would be *wrong* to remain silent. There were such things as moral obligations, after all.

"There's something you should know, Homer," she began.

He looked up with a questioning expression.

"What is it, Mother?" Dolly asked.

"Nothing. I don't suppose it's important. . . . What if Claude is dead?"

"I'd be very glad to hear it," Homer said.

"Aren't you hungry, Mother?"

"No. I think I'll go outside."

"But you've hardly touched your dinner."

"I think I'll take a walk in the garden."

Outside, she prowled up and down. A catbird followed her along the path, flitting from tree to tree, just out of sight, asking soft anxious questions. The roses, neglected for the past two days, were scattering faded petals. Swallows dipped low, snatching at insects. The garden had such a peaceful look, such a *loved* look. Gazing about her, she was forced to concede that perhaps, in arranging and nourishing these masses of bloom, this neat shrubbery, Homer had shown himself to be as much an artist —in his way—as she was.

Grace was sitting under the rose arbor at the end of the path, near the tool house. Mrs. Bigelow stood looking down at her, exasperated by her brooding attitude. "What are you mooning about?" she asked.

"Nothing."

"I should hang my head in shame, if I were you. I suppose you realize that the entire village knows what a fool you've made of yourself."

"It will give them something to talk about."

"Even your husband knows."

"And doesn't care," Grace said, "except for what people might say."

Mrs. Bigelow's exasperation vanished. She sat down. "You're mistaken if you think Raymond doesn't care. He does. You should know by now that men have queer ways of showing their feelings."

Grace looked away. "It was only because I was so damned bored. I only wanted someone to talk to."

"I know," her mother said, remembering her own married life. "I've always been fond of Raymond," she went on, "but then, of course, I don't have to live with him. I suppose he is dull. And one must admit that he hasn't made the success of his life that Homer has. However, I believe most women want husbands who are dull. They're easier to handle. Supposing you had married someone like Claude?"

"I never wanted to *marry* him," Grace said in a surprised voice.

"Perhaps you'd be good enough to explain what you did want," Mrs. Bigelow said; then, fearful that Grace would oblige, she sighed and asked, "Have I been a failure as a mother, as well?"

"As well as what? Mother, why are you sitting there feeling sorry for yourself? Everyone else is tickled to death to see the last of Claude."

"Including you?"

"Yes, including me."

"Then why are you sitting here brooding?"

"I'm not brooding. I'm thinking."

"You ought to get a job."

"To take my mind off myself? I know. That's what Dolly said. But Raymond likes living here. He doesn't want to move back to the city."

"I don't like the country," Mrs. Bigelow asserted, from habit.

"What I'd like to do," Grace said, picking a rose off the trellis beside her and twirling it between her fingers, "is open a little shop in the village. A bookshop."

"Nobody reads books any more."

"Don't be silly, Mother. Do you know that the village people have to send all the way to the city for text-books and school supplies? Raymond would like a bookshop. He could spend the afternoons there, reading. It would give him something to do—a place to go."

"You'd need money."

"Perhaps I could borrow from Homer. Or from George," Grace added, with a side glance at her mother, "if he's going to be one of the family. Is he?"

"I think I'll walk to the village," Mrs. Bigelow said, rising.

"Aren't you interested in my bookshop?"

"Yes. I think it's a good idea. I'm sure it is. I'm going for a walk."

When she walked past the house, Dolly and Homer were sitting hand in hand on the terrace. "Good news, Mother," Homer said. "I've had another call from Frank. He says they've just about given up hope of finding Claude. They traced him as far as Buffalo—at least, a man answering his description was seen boarding the New York plane there. They think he might have changed planes at New York and escaped to Mexico."

If she were ever going to tell them, now was the time, Mrs. Bigelow thought. Instead she said sharply, "What if he comes back?"

"Comes back?"

"After the fuss has died down, he might find a way.

Or he might give himself up for the satisfaction of proving that he is your Aunt Harriet's real heir."

"We'll deal with that when it happens," Homer said. "*If* it happens. I feel quite sure it will not. Claude never believed, you see, that we'd go to the police. He was all bluff. I think we can safely assume that he won't bother us again. We've cooked his goose."

You can say *that* again, Mrs. Bigelow thought, using one of George's expressions.

Homer tilted back with his hands behind his head. "Listen!" he said. Mrs. Bigelow turned, startled, but he was smiling, his eyes half closed as if he heard music. "Don't you feel it?" he asked. "The peace? The quiet? There's the seven o'clock train leaving the station. I always liked the sound of a distant train. Hear the whistle? Hear the mourning doves?"

"The house is ours again," Dolly said.

"Why are you crying?" her mother asked, frowning.

"Because I'm happy. Because all our troubles are over and we can go on being happy. I couldn't have borne it if we had been forced to give up this house." Dolly pressed her cheek to Homer's shoulder and wept in earnest, thinking of this. When she could speak again, she said, "The first time I saw this house—before we bought it— I thought, nothing bad could ever happen in that place. And I was right, you see. Everything has turned out for the best. Soon we'll all have forgotten these past few months. . . . Even Grace is beginning to like it here. She's going to open a bookshop in the village. And next year, Homer, you'll win the garden prize."

Homer bent to kiss her wet cheek.

Slobbering over one another, Mrs. Bigelow thought. She wandered down the driveway. That settles it, she told herself. I cannot ruin my own daughter's happiness simply to appease my conscience. I must keep what I know to myself.

So that problem was disposed of. Now she could think of herself, and how she would pass her remaining years. She could not, of course, stay on at Dove Cottage, knowing what she knew. The very thought chilled her.

She took the path that ran through the fields towards the village. When she reached the cemetery she sat on a lichened stone and tried to plan some sort of a future for herself. The sun dropped behind the hills. Much later, the long dusk began to fade. Perhaps I can stretch out here for the night, she thought. Sleeping in a cemetery was not nearly as frightening as spending the night in her room, where Claude might haunt her, seeking revenge for dumping all those ashes on him. She was homeless now as well as unloved. As the shadows deepened, nighthawks began to dart overhead, and there were furtive movements just beyond her vision—animals beginning their night's hunting. Before today, the prospect of being alone in the country at night would have terrified her. Fear of nature was now submerged in loneliness, and in the greater fear of going home. When an owl drifted soundlessly past her, she simply covered her eyes, waiting for the shelter of complete darkness.

I will go to the old folks' home, she decided. I will sleep here tonight and go to the old folks' home in the morning.

Comparing the life she would lead at such a place with the life she had once hoped to lead with George brought on a flood of weeping. She lay her cheek against a stone. Her tears ran into the blackened grooves of an epitaph in memory of "Eliza, beloved wife of . . ." she could not see the rest. No such epitaph would decorate her tombstone. She was doomed to die alone. It was her own fault.

She had put the welfare of others before her own happiness. That had always been her weakness, sacrificing herself for others. She felt down the neck of her dress for a handkerchief with which to dry her tears, then wiped them away with the back of her hand. She did not blame George for turning to someone else. He was human, after all, and dreaded loneliness as much as she did. In an excess of self-pity, she imagined the discomforts she would encounter at the old folks' home: sharing a bleak room with other elderly women, eating the tasteless institutional meals, being forced to take part in "activities" which she supposed included basket-weaving and other dreary pastimes. The picture was so disheartening that she sobbed aloud.

"Not crying, are you?" George asked, coming up behind her.

She lifted her blotched and swollen face, past caring what she looked like.

"Say, you *are* crying!" George patted her eyes with a handkerchief. This gesture of tenderness brought on a fresh flood. "I don't wonder you're upset," he said, holding her head against his chest. "You've had a hard time of it. I've been talking to Dolly and Homer. They told me the whole story: about Claude and his counterfeiting, and about Grace, too."

"I'm sorry about last night."

"Don't you worry about last night. Dolly told me what happened; why you forgot your date with me."

"I didn't *forget*."

"I wouldn't blame you if you had."

"I tried to telephone. Didn't Lola tell you?"

"Lola never tells me anything. She's jealous of you— of all my friends. You know what she's trying to do now?"

"What?"

"She's trying to marry me off to her mother."

"Her mother?"

"Honest! She's got her mother staying with us now—one of those mincey little fat women, not a brain in her head."

"I believe I saw her in the village this morning."

"At the supermarket? I didn't see you there. Well, anyway, if you saw her, you know what she's like. There's nothing *dignified* about her," George complained. "All she does is talk. Never stops. I haven't got a word in edgewise since she arrived. I'm getting pretty sick of it, I can tell you." He folded his handkerchief and tucked it away, for Mrs. Bigelow's tears had stopped. "I've got a good mind to move out," he said moodily. "Take an apartment in the city."

"That would be nice." Mrs. Bigelow thought it would only be nice if she were in the apartment with him. "Do you still want to marry me?" she asked.

"You mean you will?" His moon face brightened. "I'd just about given up hope."

"You said once that what you'd like to do is go off without saying a word to anyone, then send a wire saying we were on our honeymoon."

"That's what I'd like to do. I can just see Fred and Lola's faces."

"Then why don't we?"

"You mean it?" George had been put off so many times that now he could not believe she was serious.

"I'm tired of living in the country. I'd like to take a nice long trip. I'd go tonight if you'd ask me."

When George saw that she was in earnest he began with great enthusiasm to make plans. "We'll elope," he said. "We'll go—oh, anywhere. We'll pick a spot on the map and drive there tonight." He was just able, in the fast-failing light, to read his watch. "It's nine-thirty now. How long will it take you to pack?"

"Ten minutes." She did not want to be in her room for long when it got really dark.

"Let's say half an hour. Do you want to tell Dolly and Homer?"

"No. I'll leave a note."

"Well, that suits me. We won't tell a soul. I'll nip home and pack my things and bring the car around. I'll park at the end of the driveway, under that big maple tree. At ten o'clock on the dot I'll be under your window."

"We'll need a ladder."

George came back to earth. "I guess I thought I was Romeo or somebody. We'd look a fine pair of fools trying to climb down a ladder, especially with your bags." He gave an excited laugh, visualizing this. "At our age, as Lola would say. Why don't I just drop in and invite you to take a drive with me?"

"Yes. I suppose that's the sensible way." Mrs. Bigelow gave a small sigh. She had rather fancied the picture of herself descending a ladder into her lover's arms.

They walked home hand in hand. On the front porch of Dove Cottage George whispered, "How about a kiss?" She gave him a good long smack, then let herself in quietly and tiptoed upstairs.

She packed two suitcases, stacked them in a corner along with her painting equipment, fixed her face and put on her best suit. Over this she threw an old paint-smeared smock, and stole downstairs again. All her tip-toeing had been wasted. Dolly was not at home, and Homer was in the study, writing. He sat with his back to the half-closed door and did not even turn around when she passed through the hall. "That you, Mother?" he called in an absent-minded voice. "Dolly's gone over to Grace's."

Mrs. Bigelow made three trips upstairs for her luggage —which she piled beside the front steps—without disturbing him. Then she pulled a chair up to the little desk in her room to compose a farewell note. She wept a little. Dolly and Homer had tried to make her happy. They were not to blame because their efforts had failed. Perhaps I was happier than I thought, she mused, pinning the note to the pink velvet pincushion on her dresser.

At one minute to ten she went downstairs to wait for George. Homer was still writing in the study. He was bent forward with his elbows on the desk, and now and then he chewed the end of his pencil, thinking. He did not look in the least unhappy—quite the reverse, in fact— but his very contentment struck Mrs. Bigelow as touching. She felt impelled to speak to him, to offer encouragement. "I see you've taken up the literary life again," she said, pushing the door all the way open. She leaned over his shoulder and read aloud: "*Madelaine knocked on the door. 'Charles, Inspector Timmins is here,' she called. 'He wants to question you about Aunt Margaret's sudden disappearance, which took place six years ago.' After a moment Charles opened the door. He mopped his brow nervously with a white handkerchief as he motioned them inside.* That reads very well, Homer," she said kindly. "Quite a professional touch about it. I presume that Charles is not the guilty party, or you wouldn't have allowed him to act suspicious on page four. That's one of the things you must watch when you're writing a mystery story. The guilty party must appear innocent up to the last page."

"Yes, I know, Mother," Homer said patiently.

"Well, I was only trying to be helpful. After all, if we can't help one another, what's the use?"

Homer nodded without turning. He held his pencil poised above his writing pad, ready to begin again as soon as this interruption was over.

"I'm going for a drive with George," Mrs. Bigelow said. She felt that some further gesture of farewell should be made, but could think of nothing appropriate to the occasion. Her glance fell on the picture over the fireplace, her first painting, the one of the village with the houses that she now had to admit *did* resemble cows. "When I die I want you to have that picture, Homer," she said. "It may be worth a lot of money some day, when I'm famous."

"When you *die*?" Homer swivelled around. "I never thought I'd hear you admit such a possibility."

"I expect to live another twenty years, at least. I simply want you to know that when I do go, you're to have that picture."

"Thank you, Mother."

Mrs. Bigelow lingered, one hand on the doorknob, and at last Homer said, "I'm rather busy, if you'll excuse me . . ." and went back to his writing.

"Well, good-bye."

"Good-night, Mother."

She went out into the starry night. George was piling her bags on top of his own in the trunk of his car. In the pale light shed by the rustic porch lamps his face shone with excitement. "Say, aren't we the devils, though?" he said, and took her hand and led her down the steps.